The Local Lads

The Local Lads
by
Jack S. Scott

E. P. DUTTON, INC. / NEW YORK

Published in the United States by E. P. Dutton, Inc., 2 Park Avenue, New York, N.Y. 10016

Library of Congress Cataloging in Publication Data

Scott, Jack S.
   The local lads.
   "A Joan Kahn book."
   I. Title.
PS3569.C633L6   1982   813'.54   82-12805
ISBN: 0-525-24159-0

Copyeditor: Elaine Chubb

Designed by: Font 4

10   9   8   7   6   5   4   3   2   1

First Edition

The Local Lads

1

Let us agree at once: it was by lurid co-incidence that Detective Inspector Rosher became personally involved in the case. Perhaps without coincidence he would not have worked on it at all, because Detective Chief Superintendent (Percy) Fillimore was in charge, and Chief Superintendent (Percy) Fillimore never picked Inspector Rosher as second-in-command if he could help it. Indeed, he had already coopted Detective Inspector Young Alec Cruse.

Oh yes—the whole matter smacked of the lurid from the very beginning. Right on from the plane crash; which had nothing whatever to do with the case or cases.

If you enjoy seeking out the true genesis of things, you may well observe that the chain of events jangled into motion long before even that, when a man called Harold Fitter committed an armed robbery of such ferocity—he shot and wounded a cashier and took pots at policemen—that he wound up in the dock at the Old Bailey, with Inspector Rosher gone down by train to speak a police piece against him. The part Rosher had played in the arrest and the reason why, as a result, he was needed in court have no importance. Such things are police routine. What really counts as first clonk of the chain is the fact that he was there, and so was Mr.

Dunfreet of Dunfreet, Dunfreet, Hoare and Dunfreet, solicitors of the town. Working in behalf of Mr. Fitter. And that doesn't matter, either. Mr. Fitter leaves us here. Mr. Dunfreet doesn't last much longer.

There is another thing, too. If Detective Inspector Rosher had been called to the stand early in the day, he would not have met Mr. Dunfreet in the passage outside the courtroom. He came down by train, and had he been called early, would have trodden that passage long before, either to catch an early one home or to give himself a little outing in London. As it happened, he was the last speaker before the court adjourned; and as he left the stand and the judge suggested packing it in for the day, Mr. Dunfreet made a little sign. So he waited in the passage outside.

Mr. Dunfreet emerged with one of the London legal men who swirled in gown and wig, and clutched papers. "Ah, Sergeant," he said.

"Inspector," said Inspector Rosher.

"Inspector," said Mr. Dunfreet. "Yes. How are you getting back?"

"Train."

"Wondered if you'd care for a lift."

"That's very nice of you, sir."

"Not at all, not at all. Leave after dinner, what? I'm dining with Sir Geoffrey." The swirly man inclined his head, gravely, for the benefit of those who might not have known that he was Sir Geoffrey.

"Ah," said Rosher. "Yes. Well—I wasn't wanting to be too late, actually." Well, it takes about four hours by road. About the same by train.

"You won't be," Mr. Dunfreet assured him. "I flew down."

"Ah," said Rosher. "In that case, I would appreciate it."

And why not? The solicitor was known in the town as a very capable and seasoned pilot, member of the club quartered at the local field. Known, that is, to people who know these things; and that includes the police.

"Fine. Fine." The solicitor was most affable. They like to stand well with their local constabulary. "Shall we say nine o'clock? Pick you up here, have you in bed by midnight." Which might have raised an eyebrow, until one looked at Rosher.

So that was arranged. Off went Mr. Dunfreet, to dine with Sir Geoffrey at his club, or in his chambers, or somewhere; and away went Inspector Rosher, down to Fleet Street for pie, chips, and peas at a pressmen's café. This he would list against a subsistence allowance permitting meals at a higher price, being a man who would sooner have the money. As he sipped the wash-down tea, black and bitter the way he and iron-stomached men in the print trade like it, he considered the profit on his train ticket, when he privately pocketed the refund on the return half.

At nine o'clock he was transported in Sir Geoffrey's gliding Rolls-Royce, along with Mr. Dunfreet, to a small airfield in Hertfordshire; and thence into the air, sitting alongside the solicitor in a little two-seater plane.

A lovely trip they had, all the lights twinkling below, little shafts of headlights moving along, toy houses lit from within, rising moon and a million more twinkling lights above, set in deep purple. Beautiful. Until, as they flattened for touchdown on the home field, just at the point where the slow-moving panorama begins to hurtle past, Mr. Dunfreet suddenly said, "Christ!" and the bloody thing dived on its nose, half a field short of the runway.

Oh, don't worry about Rosher, he wasn't killed or anything. But Mr. Dunfreet was.

At about the time when the ambulances were leaving that field, and a uniformed policeman was settling to a chilly night of guarding the wrecked plane until it could be examined and shoveled away in the morning, two young tearaways with drink inside them weaved through the broad shopping precinct in the middle of the town, crossed the main through road, and took to the darker and at this hour deserted back streets, en route for home. They passed unnoticed. The two beat policemen who patrol here for an hour from when the pubs close were coping with an uproarious darts team, and whoever was left, if not one of the cluster urging the team to kick the bastards in the knackers, was queuing for the last bus or grappled in a shop doorway, doing it standing up and quickly, before the coppers came back. That's how it is in the shopping center, late on a Friday night. They built it to improve the quality of life.

One of these young tearaways was big and burly. He walked even when he weaved with a swagger, and they called him Billy Purvis. His oppo's name was Mike Gibbins. Slighter, shorter, with smaller muscles and a bigger brain. Not very bright, but bigger.

There is a street called Craven Terrace, and one called Gross Street. They had passed through these and were entering Wallace Street as a youth came up to the corner, going the other way. So Billy Purvis did what tearaways like to do, when they have liquor taken and come upon a hapless youth—or little man; or old man; or any man lacking firepower. Females they chi-yike or/and molest—in a dark and deserted back-street area. Billy weaved so that his shoulder barged the youth off balance as he passed, and said, "Oy—fucking watch it, mate."

This was a slight youth, and circumspect. He said, "Sorry."

"Sorry?" said Billy Purvis. "So you oughta fucking be. Barging about, knocking people over."

"Done it deliberate," said Mike Gibbins. "I seen him, I was there."

So Billy Puvis grabbed the youth by the front of his nylon bomber jacket and lugged him up on tiptoe, in order that he could say with his face an inch away from round, scared white eyes, "You done it deliberate? What you wanna do that for, going around injuring people?"

"Sorry," the lad said again. A slight, near-Welsh lilt in his voice. Billy Purvis registered him now. He said, "You're a spade. You're a fucking spade." He addressed his oppo, with indignation. "He's a fucking spade."

"Oh well," said Mike Gibbins, "that's different."

The grip on the youth's jacket tightened; jerked, swinging him off his feet and round, backed to the blank wall. No houses at this end of the road, just a wall in front of a disused manufactory. Rope they made, but nobody wants it anymore, it's all nylon. "Don't—don't—" the lad said. Even in this light you could see the whites of his eyes, the good teeth shining. It wasn't a smile he was making, his lips were drawn back in fear.

Billy Purvis reached a big hand; placed the heel against the youth's nose, squashing it flat as the kinky-haired head collided with the wall, flinching back; grinding. He said, "We don't like spades. Do we, Michael?"

"Only for supper." This was witty.

"Can't fucking stand 'em," said Billy Purvis. "What's this?" he shifted his hand, to snatch away a small locket hanging at the boy's neck. "Where'd you get this? You fucking pinched it."

"I—didn't—I—"

"Don't you fucking lie to me, spade. What are you? You're a fucking liar. Time you was taught a lesson. Ain't it? Pinching and fucking lying, we don't do that sort of thing over here."

Suddenly he stood away and began to aim kung fu kicks and karate chops, culled from TV and movies starring a cult hero who did himself such a mischief he dropped dead very young; aiming minimally wide all around the flinching body; making grabs to see the black boy snatch his genital area back so that his buttocks hit the wall, jerking him comically; going *Hah!* and *Herrh!* in the approved manner, expelling ferocious air with each blow.

"Ah-h—ah-h—" the lad went, in mortal terror. "Ah —no—please—don't—"

"Hah!" went Billy Purvis, and he jabbed two stiff fingers at the white-rolling eyes; and *"Herrh!"* as, with the youth drawn up stiff in evasion, he hit him across the extended throat, using the edge of his hand. The lad went slowly down the wall, clutching his throat and choking . . . choking . . . "It works," Billy said, delightedly. It was the first time he'd tried the brick-breaker's chop, in earnest. "It fucking works, don't it?"

"Course it fucking works," Mike Gibbins said. "Supposed to work, ain't it?" He leaned over the black boy. "When you finish spewing, nig-nog, lock up before you leave."

They walked away, leaving the boy lying there, huddled and writhing and choking; until the choking stopped and he lay still.

In the small hours of the morning, when Detective Inspector Rosher was just about stirring out of unconsciousness in his hospital bed and the two tearaways were sleeping the deep prehangover sleep (separately, they didn't live together), at about the time when a strolling insomniac walking the dog came upon the body of the black boy, a man in a small but well-equipped garage in the big city tightened the last securing bolt of a petrol tank, eased himself out from under a car tilted by a hydraulic jack, and said to a second man, standing by, "There you are. Connect up the pipes and she's done."

"Petrol's not going to damage them, is it?" the second

6

man said. A silly question, but he was very nervous. People say silly things when they are nervous.

"Not touching 'em, is it?" The first man wiped his hands on oily overalls. "Put a false bottom on the bloody thing, haven't I?" As instructed, by the man who gives the orders.

"Long as the bloody tank don't spring a leak."

"Wouldn't have put it back on if it would, would I?" the overalled man said. "Wouldn't be such a twat, would I? What's it all for, anyway?"

"You just do the job. That's what you're paid for."

"Long as I don't get lumbered." The mechanic swapped spanners and prepared to roll himself back under the car, lying on his little trolley. "Ten minutes, we can go home to bed."

"Not me," the other man said. "I've got to drive it." Back to town, in readiness for tomorrow.

2

When Inspector Rosher woke up, he found the face of a pretty West Indian nurse swimming about above him. The first words he said, at five o'clock in the morning, were, "I didn't do it, Mum."

"Lie still, Mr. Rosher," the nurse said, in that attractive lilting accent. "I've rung for the doctor."

"What what what?" said Rosher. His eyes were connecting the head to a body. As pretty as the face, no doubt, under that starched uniform. It was bending over him. "What doctor?"

"Dr. Spenlowe. He'll be here in a jiffy."

"Jiffy? Jiffy?" Rosher said; and added the classic cliché that springs unbidden to the lips when faculties bonked clean out of the carcass come woozelling back in again. "Where am I?"

"St. Barnolph's hospital. You just don't move, now. Not till the doctor's seen you."

The voice of an incompletely castrated sergeant major spoke from the foot of the bed in which, he had just discovered, he was lying. "All right, Nurse?"

Rosher squinted. Close by the bed, beyond a heavily plastered leg raised in a sling, stood a tall and angular lady in starch. The pretty nurse was saying, "Yes, Sister. I've rung for Dr. Spenlowe."

"Good. Good." Something of a baritone was left in

the chest notes. "There is a—er—telephone call for you. It's in my office." Presumably she meant the telephone was, left off the hook.

"For me?" The pretty girl sounded surprised.

"Yes. The—er—police."

"Police?" Surprise deepened. That leg, Rosher found, was his. "What the police want me for? I haven't done nothing."

"It's about—I think it's about your brother."

"My brother? He hasn't done nothing either. Has he?"

"They will explain," Sister said. "Go along, I'll wait for the doctor."

Who hung my bloody leg up there? thought Rosher, indignantly; and he went to sleep again.

By midafternoon his brain was reseated, and he had visitors. They'd have been held at bay for a day or two, no doubt, had he been a civilian; but a taken-out detective leaves the brew glubbing, and other cooks must rush to the pot if the bubbles start hissing over the brim.

Two of Rosher's cases bubbled up, one while he lay unconscious and one as he blew on soup, spooned for him by a Chinese nurse who seemed to have replaced the West Indian girl. She received it from a Pakistani lady who was wheeling a great tureen of it about, on a trolley. Well may a man ask, waking today in a British hospital: Where am I?

So two detectives came. Their names do not matter, they merely looked in to seek guidance before expressing sympathy and galloping off, to effect arrests Rosher would have been making had he not plunged with a whop into that field. Nothing very big, just a man who waggled it outside the Princess Elizabeth School for Girls (the maiden who shopped him to her mum had a hard time of it afterward; it was better than biology classes) and another with an attic filled with stolen bicycles. He was only looking after them, he said. For a friend. A different friend from the one who left him lumbered last time, with all them color telly sets.

Then the chief constable arrived. This was a courtesy visit, paid by a courteous leader concerned for the well-being of everyone under his command. This man actually liked Rosher, it was he who'd found a way to restore him to inspector rank after the fierce old buzzard who preceded him bust the man down and rode him toward the exit, all for an ill-judged grab at the mammary protuberances of a publican's wife who had had them grabbed before, God knows, and come to no harm by it.

This new chief constable, younger, smoother (especially about the head), and sleeker, informed the injured inspector that he was lucky, really, to have sustained no more than a broken ankle, severe bruising, and a bash on the black hat that did not even fracture the skull when he pitched into the windscreen, held from going through it by his seat belt; because Mr. Dunfreet had broken his neck and was dead. To which Rosher, leg slung like a great white sausage and his tenpenny-piece tonsured short-back-and-sides haircut hidden under a turban of bandage, said, "Ah. Hrrmph. Pity."

He slept again after the chief left, awaking in the early evening as walking patients from the open wards settled to "Coronation Street" in the little lounges where the color televisions flickered, placed there by the Friends of St. Barnolph's. Caused a lot of medical lapses, those sets, from stressful argument over which program should be watched.

His own bed stood alone in a small annex to the main ward; the privacy afforded coming not so much by privilege as by necessity. A detective cannot discuss what he must discuss with colleagues in pursuance of duty, under the avid eyes and ears of sufferers bored to the dentures with paperback books, black grapes, bloody Lucozade, and the BBC squeezed through earphones. Everybody, in health and out, is fascinated by the detective. Except detectives, and those who marry them.

The West Indian girl was back, bringing him a cup of tea. Very quietly, arriving with it just as he awoke, as if she had a microchip sensor inside which told her he was about to do it. Perhaps they have, these days. As she eased him to a position enabling him to drink, the door opened and in came Detective Inspector Young Alec Cruse; who looked at her with eyebrows risen and said, "Oh. Hello again, Miss Holness."

"Hello," the girl replied, soft-voiced. She settled the pillow behind Rosher's aching back.

"Didn't realize you were looking after our—er—our Mr. Rosher." Plainly, Cruse hesitated on the edge of saying "our friend," and drew back. Not because he felt enmity toward Rosher—he felt enmity for no one, this was a young man with a rather nice nature—but friends they were not, and alas could never be. More than the generation gap and widely differing temperaments stood between.

"I just come back on duty," the pretty nurse said. Her skin had a lovely, dusky sheen to it, a sort of delicate bloom. And she made a soft rustle when she walked, as she did now, in sensible shoes, out of the room and away.

Cruse watched her go, wearing the smile many people said was handsome. He couldn't see why, himself. Not that it bothered him. He lowered his six-foot-two onto the small chair by Rosher's bedside and said, when she was no more than a clack receding along the corridor, "Poor kid. Bit hard on her, isn't it?"

"What is?" In his turban, when he stretched his lips forward to sip, Rosher became a dead ringer for a Hindu ape, working in a telly commercial for tea.

"I've just been talking to her." The necessity for doing so was what brought the young man to the hospital. He might, without it, have called upon the injured Blubbergut at some time, as others from the station would, whether they liked him or not. A matter of esprit de corps. But he sat here now because after he left Matron's office upstairs, where he talked with the girl, he thought: While I'm here, I might as well look at the old bastard.

"What's she been up to?"

"Not her, it's her brother. He was knocked off last night."

Rosher's eyes came up from his tea in surprise. One of them nestled in the purplest shiner since the days when he was All-England police boxing champion, three years running, in the heavyweight division. "Knocked off? Murdered?"

"Looks like it, yes. Corner of Wallace Street, he lived there with her and the mum. Could have been a fight gone wrong, he'd had his throat mashed in. The little sods sling these karate chops about, half the time they don't know what they're doing. Look at that one in April, Jubilee Crescent." This was a lad who inadvertently broke his brother's neck, using an identical chop. Went *Hah!* as he did it.

"Mmm," said Rosher. "Mm. Seems a nice girl."

"Yes. The boy seems to have been quite a decent lad. No bother, no late-night fighting. Didn't like fighting, by her account. And her mum's. Bit timid. Anyway, somebody did him last night. On the way home from a reggae party. I'm on it, with Percy."

So here it is, the crux coincidence that nudged Rosher into the case. If he'd had a different nurse, no personal involvement would have come to him. Had he not been hors de combat, had he been working, he would have known of the murder only as an incident of last night, he'd have watched progress from a distance. Never, never, never, given any choice at all, would Chief Superintendent (Percy) Fillimore have chosen him to act main support. And the nurse would never have done what she did.

"Any leads?" he asked.

"Not really, no. Nobody saw it. No dabs, he was wearing a nylon jacket. Somebody grabbed it, but it didn't take. No other injuries, just a bump on the back of the head, probably when he fell back against the wall."

"No motive?"

"The girl doesn't know of anybody who might have wanted to do him. Nor does his mother. And the kids at the party are clean, they all alibi each other. He left early, on his own. Well—early compared with the rest of 'em, some of them were still keeping it up when I got there. All West Indians. Bradshaw Road." Bradshaw Road is where most of the town's small immigrant population lives.

"Mm. Well—doesn't sound too complicated. What time, about half past eleven?"

"About then, the quack reckons." No need to ask how the other man knew. Every policeman knows what time the pubs turn out, and how much gratuitous assault takes place in the time soon after.

"Some of the herberts, on the way home. Poke around the pubs a bit, you'll soon turn 'em up."

"That's what I'm on now," said Young Alec. "Just stopped in for a word with the girl." He added quickly, "And to see how you were doing, of course. Bit of a do, that was, wasn't it?"

"I don't remember much about it." Only the solicitor saying Christ, the rushing world changing position, and a bloody great flash of light. Then I was in here.

"No, I suppose you wouldn't. Plane's a write-off. So's poor old Dunfreet, I expect you know."

"Uh-huh." Old? The bloke couldn't have been more than forty-five.

"Her name's Holness, by the way. Jennifer Holness.

Your nurse. Well"—up came the six-foot-two from the chair—"I'd better be getting along."

He was buttoning his coat with relief. At least there'd been something to bridge the terrible awkwardness he always felt in the presence of Old Blubbergut since he, detective sergeant then and assistant to Rosher on the day when he grasped the publican's wife, had, willy-nilly, to say what he'd seen, at the inquiry that bust the inspector down. Almost immediately after, his embarrassment had been increased by a complete reversal in status, when he found himself elevated to fill the establishment gap left by Rosher's downgrading and given Rosher's old office, while the erstwhile inspector worked out the time left before his pensioning off chained to a sergeant's desk in the general office. The fierce old Chief meant to destroy him; and the sure way to do it was to deny him the active fieldwork that was his true métier, and to imprison him among the paper work, which he hated, as do all good CID men.

Cruse's rightful pleasure in his own promotion—it was, in fact, thoroughly deserved—had been and still was undermined by the nagging belief (he was a modest young man) that in some way it came to him as reward for grassing. Or because the old Chief knew that this upping and downing above all would humiliate Old Blubbergut. It did, of course; but what could the young man do about it? You cannot refuse promotion, in a police force, especially one ruled by a despot of rare force and fury. Dammit, you work for promotion all your life.

Things had eased a little with Rosher's reelevating. At least they were now equal in rank, the gorilla man's pride and manhood restored, in some measure, by the infinitely more charitable and sensitive new chief constable, who respected his integrity and dogged methods—outmoded, true, but still surprisingly effective—and even seemed to like him. The damage was done, though. What lay between them would never pass away.

So Young Alec finished buttoning his coat and clamped onto his thick dark hair a felt hat of the type favored, for some reason, by the school of younger detectives that does not gump about like a clutch of wino dropouts. He did not need it, with all that hair, and it didn't really become him; but where is freedom if a man cannot clap on his poll a felt hat of whichever type he chooses? "Well," he said, "I'll be off."

"Uh-huh." If the young man's hat did nothing for him, Rosher's bandage did even less. It brought out the gorillaness of his features, it gave him the look of being dressed for a circus act. He would juggle bananas or ride a bicycle, or something. There'd be no dignity in it.

"See you, then." Cruse made his smile again.

"Uh-huh," said Rosher; and he added, stiffly because he always found difficulty in expressing appreciation, "Nice of you to drop in."

Young Alec covered his own awkwardness with a light tone, holding his smile. "Well—not every day a bloke plows in an airplane, is it? Had to see what it does to you." And he left.

Unable to sit up, Rosher drained the cup of tea and rested it on his belly. There was pain in his leg, he ached from bruising, and his head thumped dully; but physical pain had never bothered him. When a man takes policing for a career and boxing for a second activity, knowingly or unknowingly he states his indifference to it. Psychologists might say that he invites it, for kinky reasons known only to his subconscious mind; that he finds pleasure in it. Certainly this man lay now quite contentedly, sinking into a sort of peaceful drowsiness; possibly experiencing this kinky pleasure, or from reaction, or because of drugs pumped into him at some stage. Hospitals, receiving a carcass, immediately inject it. The effect lingers.

He came from a doze to find the coffee-tinted nurse

quietly removing his cup and saucer. He went, "Ahh. Hmm. Hah," the formless sounds people make when they start out of dozing.

"It's all right," her soft voice said. "I'll just take these away." Her slim brown hands lifted the cup and saucer, placed them on the bedside locker. Inevitably, because nurses cannot resist it, she began to straighten the coverlet on his bed, to ease him down, to plump up his pillows. Then she picked up the crockery and turned to leave.

He said, "I'm—er—sorry to hear about your brother."

"Yes," she said, very quietly. "Yes. Thank you."

Policemen, long saturated in procedure, become tightly bound to a certain approach. Automatically he added, "Any idea who might have done it?"

"I've already said I haven't." Now her voice was almost brusque, so far as the warm tone permitted. "To your friend."

"Sorry," he said. Not often he did that. "Thought I might be able to help."

She moved away, carrying the cup; turned when she got to the door, and her black eyes were brimming with tears. "How can you help? You can't bring him back."

"Ah. No. But I know most of the villains in town. Tearaways, yobbos."

"If you don't mind, I don't want to talk about it." Quite haughty now, the voice and the stiffly upright stance. Self-contained, self-controlled, giving him the snub direct. Only the brimming eyes gave away the pain.

"Hmmmph," said Rosher. She left the room, taking the cup, the saucer, and her soft rustle. He closed his eyes again.

Later on this same evening the souped-up tampered-with jalopy left the point where it had been stowed in town after return from the big city, and nosed through the suburbs, out to the bypass that runs through good country back to that city; this side of which, it cuts under the motorway. Nobody noticed it particularly. No reason why they should, it was merely a seven-year-old semibanger of a type stamped out by the hundreds of thousands until the model was scrapped, two years ago. Nothing in the engine note, at built-up-area speeds, to indicate an inappropriate unit under the tinny bonnet. No sign that brakes, clutch, steering were all freshly adjusted, no hint of a false bottom fitted to the petrol tank so skillfully as to defy detection even close up.

The only part of this careful jigging intended for definite use was that false bottom. Precaution only, the mechanical tinkering. Nobody was going to flag down a little old jalopy going about its lawful business, and it would be away before the roadblocks were properly set up. But good planning takes into account the unexpected; and when the brighter bent put a car on the job, they ensure that if necessary it will take off with a zoop, able to match or outrun whatever comes after it. And they put a skilled driver behind the wheel. With an oppo to back him up; because something might happen to him, too.

This car had a good driver. At the wheel was Mike Gibbins, smaller and brighter of the two tearaways who last night did up a spade boy and thought no more about it. They were not thinking of it now, he and Billy Purvis sitting beside him as he took the car out from the town and onto the bypass. Didn't know the boy was dead. Neither of them read newspapers unless they fancied a leer at page 3, where the tits are, or needed to study the football page. There are better displays of crumpet than the public press can offer, and this was the cricket season. So there you are. Of the other media, only the local radio station reported the matter; and they didn't listen to that.

In point of fact, these two lads would seem to give

weight to the argument that talent has nothing whatever to do with intellect; that it exists in some form even in people who seem, intellectually, little better than cretins. Aye, and blossoms fully, once the subject stumbles on vocation, only when vision is narrowed by an absorption that excludes all else.

Their shared passion was for mechanical transport, particularly the driving thereof. They cut their teeth early, on a motor resurrected from a scrapyard and given new life by sheer instinct. They bashed about stock car circuits, cherishing the ambition to drive, someday, Formula One cars on to fame and glory. Both had been given trials by the big-city speedway club; but Billy Purvis was not quite at home on cinders, and Mike Gibbins, who almost broke a long-standing lap record the very first time he rode the track alone, flinched from cornering tight when three other maniacs shot with him out of the gate and dived sliding with engines bellowing for inside berth on the first bend. A major part of the speedway rider's equipment is sheer nerve. He just didn't have enough of it.

But driving skill he had in abundance; and only minor form: no real police trouble. Neither of them had. They were done once for selling an unroadworthy banger—they tarted up and flogged old cars, as a curbside business, having no premises to work from—and each had been knocked for little things like speeding; but in the files of genuine malefactors they did not appear.

It made of them a desirable property, in certain quarters, because this lack of form was due far more to pure luck than to shining honesty. There are talent spotters among the bent; and the man who owned the garage to which this car would be delivered eventually, together with the scrapyard at the back, was a very naughty man indeed. He knew of them, and had tested them out well on minor jobs—a vanload of stolen cigarettes, a bootful of hot whiskey, even a truck packed with highly desirable fur coats deflected from its rightful destination. Now he was using them for the big one. Mind you, he did not tell them it was big. But he raised the money.

So all they knew, as they drove out to the bypass and turned onto it, was that the adrenaline gurgled pleasantly in their veins and the work promised to be lucrative, by their standards. Mike said, as they aimed toward the big city, "He's given us a bloody good car here. Sod of an engine in her. Wonder what she'd do, flat out?"

"Hold her back, for Christ's sake," said Billy. The needle was flickering up to sixty, the engine was beginning to bay. "We don't wanna get knocked."

"No sweat, the speed limit here's seventy."

"Fucking bangers don't piss along at seventy," Billy said, "with a fucking great tiger in the tank."

Mike eased his throttle. The baying ceased as the speed dropped until they were pottering along nicely. He said, "Wonder what it is? The tickle. Wonder what the job is?"

"Who fucking cares? Upped the fucking bread, ain't he? Few more like this one, we can get our own garage."

"Build our own Formula One."

"If you don't piss your half up against the wall."

"Hark who's fucking talking. Stop in a lay-by somewhere, let me take her over, get the feel of her."

Ah, the heady dreams of youth. It costs tens of thousands to build a Formula One car. Hundreds of thousands, to race it. Well—who would impose limits to the high-flying ambition of a young man, when the adrenaline is flowing, tickle is in the offing, and he has connections? Chatting very amiably, they traveled on, changing places on the way; until Mike said, "Aye up—there's the turnoff," and they drove along a lane to the rendezvous point.

3

He was a big man, the man who owned the garage. Elton Vennor, his name was, and he operated on two levels: as solid, respectable businessman, and as controlling force and planning brain behind a major percentage of the crime statistics for the area.

Not beatings-up and rapings, not flashings and malicious woundings and the annexation of old people's life savings, they having opened the door to the gasman. He was not concerned in all the mucky little delinquencies that ebb and flow around any human settlement—this one no less than most, so that many of its longer-service policemen were by now persuaded that God worked hard for six whole days, and came up with a bloody great sewer. No: his were the bigger matters. One might even say, the cleaner.

He controlled a consortium. Not a gang, a consortium. A loose connection spreading far beyond the town, with contacts even as far as the Smoke; operating individually for the most part, because petermen, burglars, bank and sub-post-office raiders, and plain regular villains must work consistently, having commitments to meet even as you and I; coming together when he called. Not all of them, just the specialists he had chosen for the particular job. Always, when he whistled they came. It was bound to be something good.

This was the best ever, surpassing by far, if they brought it off, the bank job at Altrincham when they cut through from next door, the sudden snatch in Hatton Garden, the cool cheek of the workmen (and he was one) who carried their own oxyacetylene equipment into an office building at Birmingham on a Friday afternoon and out again on the Monday morning, together with all the boodle from a jeweler's vault under the adjoining building. Many, many jobs like that. And nobody ever shopped him, he was too well respected. Fed too many people.

He sat now in a saloon car beside another good driver, who would have driven the souped-up jalopy but for the fact that he had accumulated too much form. One of the problems shared by the hierarchy bent is getting good help not too familiar to the police. Hence the constant talent spotting. So he sat in this saloon car parked in a lay-by area, watching as an unobtrusive family production model drew into the lay-by opposite, stopping behind a long flatbed truck already there, and he said to this good driver, "Good. Good. There's Plonker. That's everybody." He'd watched the souped-up jalopy go by some time ago, Billy Purvis at the wheel.

"Yeah. Good," said the driver. His name was Arnold Gutte. Isn't that extraordinary? He told everybody, and strove desperately to believe, that it derived from the Germanic Gotte, as in *Gott in Himmel* or *mitt uns;* but he remained bedeviled by doubt. One does, in a case like this. "What time's the truck come along?"

"Soon. Soon." The boss man spoke soothingly. One of his great attributes as a leader was his ability to feel the adrenaline flow in his troops, to tolerate stupid questions asked by quite intelligent men under the influence of it, and to soothe while continuing to impose discipline. The other great thing that won him respect: he led from the front. There was no compulsion for him to be here at all; but he loved it, the kick of action. He loved it, and the bent admired him for it. What risks there were, he shared.

Now he sat back, relaxed and easy with the small transmitter/receiver in his lap, waiting with the blood moving pleasantly in him. They all waited: Arnold Gutte at the wheel beside him; the driver of that car in the lay-by opposite; two men in the cab on the flatbed truck. All stolen, these vehicles. Chosen long ago, borrowed earlier today. But not from the town. Too local.

Four minutes, five; and the little set gave tongue against a background of static. "Father," it squawked. "Hopwood Lane roundabout."

This was all, by arrangement. When the security van approached the roundabout half a mile away, the passenger in a car that nosed out from a side road to fall in behind broadcast this brief message to Father. All the waiting men received it. "Right," said the good leader. "Here we go."

He pulled on his balaclava helmet and rolled the visor down over features that were by no means ugly, although just beginning to go jowly because he lived well. Arnold Gutte, who was a good deal uglier, favored the ever-popular nylon stocking, in gunmetal gray. The car opposite drew out gently and joined very light traffic going toward the Geering Corner roundabout, which is nearer than Hopwood Lane. Just up the road, in fact, a few hundred yards from here. The men in this car wore at this juncture felt hats and bare faces. They would mask up at the roundabout, for the ride back.

There is no denying it, the timing was beautiful. And not by chance, don't think it. Meticulous planning went into this, there had been dry runs and stopwatches clicked. You can time a vehicle very accurately over six hundred yards, if you know what speed it will travel at; and you set that by selecting a bot-

tleneck section of road and sending along it at the
appropriate moment a wagon too wide to be passed
until the roundabout approach, when it turns off left
and trundles sedately away from the scene of action.
And you clear the road behind by having a tractor,
coming out of a field on the near side pulling a long
agricultural flat, get stuck across the bottleneck. It can
shuffle back and forth for as long as you need it, trying
to turn; and every time it backs it releases whatever
traffic has built up going away from you, and this
traffic, impatiently letting in the clutch, effectively
prevents cars coming toward you from steering around.

In other words, you block just one side of the road.
You don't block both. Well, the last thing you want is to
be impeded by a traffic jam on your side, when you
come hurtling along.

So the car from the lay-by reached the roundabout
just as the wide truck did, from the opposite direction.
The truck went left; the car following it (security
guards in there) came straight on, followed by the
boodle van; the car with the villains in steered right
around the island and fell in behind, at a discreet
distance.

From the lay-bys where the flatbed truck and the big
man's car waited, engines awake now, you can see the
Geering Corner roundabout. That impeding truck had
served two purposes: it had held the victim back while
the uninhibited traffic ahead raced on, to leave the
stretch of road clear. Only the security firm van approached, its escort before and the villain car behind.
"Let's go," said Elton Vennor, to Arnold and his little
radio set.

From now, the entire action took no more than a
minute. A piece of the proverbial cake. But do not be
tempted to try it, unless you have the connections.
Vennor himself was not sole proprietor here, he was
working with London associates, who for a hefty cut
had insinuated a man of their own into the boodle van.

Never mind how, some secrets are best kept in the family. It was this man—another skilled mechanic—who had been able to fix a delayed breakdown, so that the van was here on a Saturday evening, long after it should have been at rest, and when traffic on the bypass is light. At rush hour it's murder. No problem is insoluble, if you have a brain and know the right people, and have the cut to offer them. It doesn't come cheap, but it is money well invested. Saves gunplay, or nicking the van (always dodgy), or—dodgier still—trying to cut your way in on a public highway.

The guns were there; but nobody needed to fire one. What happened was this:

The car driven by Arnold traveled only about twenty yards before it stopped, as the elongated flatbed truck drove out straight across the road, right in the path of the escort car; completely blocking the two carriageways. Almost before the guard car and the van squealed to a halt, the two men were out of that cab and were pressing the muzzles of sawn-off shotguns against the car windows. The villain car shot up, alongside the van, and out tumbled two more rogues, to do the same thing here.

Well—toughened glass it may be, and all sorts of claims made by the manufacturers, who fire pistols at it; but men not all that well paid tend to wonder, under these circumstances, what happens when you shove a shotgun right onto it and blast away. They think of their children, they think of wives and sweethearts, either or both; and they sit tight.

So nobody fired a gun. The back doors of the van simply opened and there was the planted guard. Simple. All he brought was a few canvas bags as he raced across the road and into the back of Vennor's car. Whereupon Arnold put his foot down.

That left one car and a great big truck, the command car on its way: squealing the curve of the roundabout and straight on, past that tractor and trailer, which backed sufficiently to let it by and then all the way into the field, where the driver jumped down and walked via the farmyard to his car. They found the farmer and his wife later, by the way, trussed up in the farmhouse.

It must be understood that the second car did not hang about. It took off, it is true, a few seconds later than the other, but in good order and according to plan. By the time the planted guard was in the back of Vennor's car, one man from the other had upped the bonnet of the escort car and ripped out a handful of wires. He then boarded the villains' car, his co-workers bundling in with him while keeping their guns pointed; and the car backed—had to, being alongside the van: couldn't have made the turn otherwise—skreeked around in a loop, and shot away, turning right at the roundabout. Add a little confusion when you can, beetle off in different directions. There's a network of lanes, back of the bypass.

Nothing left now but the flatbed truck; and this did not belong to Vennor or to any of them, so it was extremely dispensible. No fingerprints—no fag ends —nothing. They all wore gloves, and you don't do this sort of work with a Woodbine glued to the lower lip. Tire marks, yes. Try to match that lot up. Ordinary Dunlops, worn by millions.

A few minutes later, the first car arrived in the barn where Mike Gibbins and Billy Purvis waited with the souped-up jalopy. This barn, part of a tumbledown and deserted farm, is approached by those lanes through good, screening woods. It has been used before, notably on St. Barnolph's Day last, when naughty men gathered here before setting off to annex baubles belonging to a nasty little millionaire called Sir Roland Goyt; which raid ended in violence, and death, and the act of heroism that clinched the reelevation of Rosher, who did not know at the time that he was being a hero.

Almost before the car halted, the three men inside were out. Vennor said to the young tearaways, cool as a cucumber and wearing his pleasant smile, "Hello, lads. Get the petrol cap off." He had taken possession of the canvas bags. "Then wait outside. Keep watch."

The blood pumping up in them—it was, after all, their first job in company, and Arnold still wore his stocking—the apprentices hurried to do as they were told. Arnold, when they were gone, inserted a clever funnel into the petrol aperture. It locked in, well down and out of sight, to a second aperture made in the side of the ingress pipe, where a bypassing pipe led straight down to that cunningly wrought cache under the tank.

The big man stepped forward. There was not great bulk in the canvas sacks; value in the jewelry trade does not necessarily come by the kilo. The tapes securing the necks were already untied, because he had not been twiddling his thumbs on the short dash here. Without even a peek at the contents he poured them into the funnel.

In a very few minutes the whole of the loot was down there under the tank, and Arnold was using a grappling tool, designed by Vennor and constructed in his own workshop, to fit a plug over that out-of-sight aperture, so that if the car needed to top up with petrol—not that it would; but again, plan for the unexpected—none of it would go down the wrong way. Would not damage the cargo if it did; but wouldn't run the car, either. And it would complicate recovery, splashing all over the place when the false bottom came off. You couldn't use the drain plug, it passed straight into the real tank.

The second car did not linger. It arrived now; but only to collect the guard. No reason for it to stay, and the sooner away the better. Five now in that car—and all the shotguns. But waiting along the road was the third car—the one that made the "Father" radio call, and then fell out. Into this would transfer the London men and the shotguns. They'd all be back in London in a few hours, clear of here before things began to buzz.

Nor did Vennor hang about. As soon as the sacks were empty he called the lads back in and said, "Now, you know what to do, don't you?"

Mike spoke for both. "Wait till after dark, drive easy to town."

"And?" said Vennor.

"And what?"

"Don't go throwing money about."

"Oh—yeah. Well, we know that, don't we?"

"Good. And listen: no cockups. I shall be very, very angry if we have any cockups."

"We all fucking will," said Arnold Gutte. He was removing false number plates from the first car. Easy enough, they spring-clipped on. "And we can be very nasty. Very rough."

"Off we go, then. And don't take your gloves off. Right?" Very important, this. Somebody took a glove off, and look what happened to the Great Train Robbers. "Not until you leave here."

"Don't worry, Mr. Vennor," said Mike. "We know the form." Nobody equals the tyro for confidence.

"Just so you remember it." The big man's smile flashed once again as he got back into the car. Somehow, he injected a deal of menace into it. Arnold Gutte tossed the number plates to young Billy Purvis and ducked in behind the wheel. "Shove them up in the rafters," he said. The car rolled away, headed not back to the bypass but on through quiet lanes, to enter the town from a different direction. Arnold said as they went, "I'm not too happy about leaving a couple of herberts with it. I mean—not like a packet of sherbet, is it? I mean—we don't even know 'em, do we? Well— *you* do. But I don't. Nobody else does."

"That's the whole point, Arnie. Nobody does. No

form, not even a signature in the probation book. And the jalopy looks just right for them. It's got its own license, got its own plates. Everything clean."

"Got that fucking great engine, though, ain't it?" As I know—I drove it back from the city last night.

"They're only going a few miles, aren't they? At legal speeds. Why should anybody spot the engine? Even if they did—so they're trying it out for stock car racing. They're known on all the tracks."

"Long as the Old Bill don't get after 'em."

"Nothing to give yourself ulcers about. I'm telling you, they're clean. They don't even know what they're carrying. And if they *do* have to run—I've seen 'em drive, and they know what to do." And well aware that Arnold's concern had some measure of professional jealousy in it, he added, "Mind you, I'd sooner have used you, but—well—you know how it is." You've got form, son. That's why you get out and take a bus when we come out of these lanes, and I drive on alone.

"There's always Foxy Foxwell," Arnold said.

"Foxy's inside," Vennor told him gently. "Believe me, I know what I'm doing. Nobody's going to expect two little yobbos to be on a job like this, the Old Bill'll be sorting out the known lads. And not here—they'll be looking around the city, around the Smoke, they won't see anybody here they'll think is big enough to handle it. By the time they hot it up here—*if* they ever do, the way we've fixed it—it'll all be gone without trace."

"Well—you're the boss," said Arnold.

"Yes. I'm the boss."

Left in the barn, the two tearaways did as they had been instructed. They ascended the rickety ladder to the loft section and shoved those number plates up behind the enormous rafters. No need to hide them too cleverly, because nobody was likely to come here searching until the bulldozers arrived at some future time; by when the matter would be ancient history. No sense in leaving them downstairs in full view of wandering tramps or the odd swain and maiden looking for somewhere to couple; but if they removed and broke up the ladder, the rafters should be safe enough.

This they did, enjoying it: pulling one side away from the rungs and wrenching out some of the rungs themselves from both ends; flinging these far away into bushes at the back of the barn. The main part they left under litter beside the old, roofless house, part of the general clutter of rot and rust that surrounds such unloved places. Even if somebody sought out and reassembled this main structure, unless they somehow gathered all those rungs they'd need to be a gifted acrobat to mount it.

When the job was done, Mike said, "That's it, then. All we do now is wait."

"Got a tin of glue in the car," said Billy. "Want a sniff?"

"Don't be a twat. What you wanna bring that for? We ain't getting high on a job for him. Not the first fucking proper one."

Billy was grinning. "Only joking, wadden I? Whajjer think I fucking am? Could do with a fag, though."

"No you fucking couldn't." Strictly no smoking. Vennor's orders. "We sit where we can see out, like Vennor said." And if anybody comes, he did not have to add, we let in that fiery clutch and go like the clappers.

They spent the next hour keeping watch while the sun went down over the woods and fields and all the green countryside. When it was nearly dark, Mike said, "Right. Reckon we can go now, don't you? I'll run the jalopy out, you get the broom."

So they reopened the great barn doors, and while Mike drove the car out onto the track Billy took up an aged, patchily molted yard broom found here among the junk and swept around a little: not cleaning the place up, but simply to remove any surface traces the cars might have left. When this was done he leaned the broom back where he found it, against an old mangold crusher all seized up with rust, and joined his oppo. The car drove away, without lights. No problem, there was enough left of daylight to show the track leading down to the gate into the lane. Neither lad had any idea that Elton Vennor was already in the cottage hospital, just along the corridor from where Detective Inspector Alfred Stanley Rosher lay.

The first man to know what happened to Elton Vennor was Arnold Gutte, and it gave him a terrible shock. He left the car just before the lane emerges into the main road. Not the bypass road now humming with police activity, but the other one, the A road that leads into town from the opposite side, and through it and on, over the hills and far away. Vennor got out to take the wheel and said, "Right. Half an hour to wait for your bus. Keep out of trouble, I'll see you tomorrow. Went well, didn't it?"

"Bleeding doddle," Arnold said. "Long as the lads don't cock something up." He did not really believe they would—if Vennor vouched for them on a job of this magnitude, they had to be all right—but he had driven a great deal of loot in his time. It irked him that he was not driving this. Say what you will, he was known as one of the best in the caper, veteran of many a fast getaway. Stayed ahead of the Old Bill once all the way from the Smoke to bloody nearly York, where he lost 'em in the lanes near the village of Askham Richard. And that's what he meant: you need experience. For instance: what would have happened that day, if he hadn't thought or bothered to fill the tank? He was only supposed to be going to Barnet.

Vennor walked around the car and shut himself in behind the wheel. He gave a small wave and drove away. Arnold watched until the car vanished around the bend, and then thought: I could do with a pint. The Dun Cow's just along by the bus stop.

Well, it was safe enough. No need to go to ground, when a job has gone well. Better, in fact, to be seen by as many people as possible in public places decently away from the scene of the malpractice, so long as you remember to take your nylon stocking off. He'd done that, it was in his pocket.

The next half-hour, during which after a short walk he downed two pints of bitter, were most enjoyable. Comes elation after a successful conclusion to long and concentrated endeavor. The actor knows it, and every man of imagination who has dreamed a thing and dared to bring it off. The man who invented the water closet would have known it, when he pulled the chain and found the bloody thing worked. And Arnold knew it. Had known it all his working life, but never so strongly as this, because tonight saw him rich. Well— comfortably off. Forever. He sat in the pub and enjoyed, while the beer lubricated him beautifully. Excitement and action, they build a helluva thirst.

He stepped out from the pub as the bus arrived at the stop outside—how seldom are bus stops so thoughtfully situated—and boarded it. All seemed cheery, fellow travelers, conductor, world going by bathed in late gold-shine, the humped back of the driver, et al. All does, when you are in exalted and purely benevolent mood, with a couple of pints of bitter nestled in the gratified stomach. It's a condition to watch, warily; because Fate is a tricky bitch, and if she can, she will now knock you sideways, with a vicious back-swipe of her bony-knuckled hand.

She did it to Arnold. The bus slowed suddenly, at a traffic jam. When it had crawled on far enough a young policeman could be seen. He was on the offside. On the nearside—right out across the town-bound lane, really—was the front end of a truck as long and tough-

girdered as the one used to block the bypass, the cab
door swinging open. A car stood twisted, all the front
end buckled and jammed under the high chassis, immediately abaft the front wheel. An ambulance stood
by. They were just loading somebody into it, supine on
a stretcher.

"Jesus Christ!" said Arnold, quite loudly; and rose in
his seat, in spite of the notice warning him not to do it,
so rapidly that he whacked his head on the parcel rack.
It sat him down again.

Well might he rise and whack his head. He knew
that car, didn't he? Not long ago, he got out of it.

4

What some call coincidence, others see as the Hand of Fate. The bedding down of Elton Vennor in a hospital already containing Inspector Rosher should be seen as a waggle of the latter rather than the former. Coincidence, perhaps, that he ran into a lorry so soon after Rosher fell into a field; but what the hell—accidents happen all the time; and once they have, in this town, unless the unfortunate is delivered straight to the morgue there is only one place to take him. And that is St. Barnolph's Cottage Hospital.

Rosher, of course, knew nothing of the other man's arrival, and would have felt no particular interest had he been told. If he knew Vennor at all it was because a copper tends to know every entrepreneur in his area. It's part of the trade. But unless the man works and resides actually upon his particular patch, the copper will rarely know him well. Until he falls foul of the law. If he does that, he becomes forever very notable.

Vennor came to the town ten years ago, after his one spell of porridge. With money stashed from the car caper that sent him in, he started a small garage, and by genuine hard work had built a solid business. Three of them. If the hard work took place on two levels— isn't it often the case? How else do politicians get rich? He had no form in the town.

So they brought him in and put him into the Casualty Ward; and while the police notified his wife the doctor got to work, setting him up for blood transfusion and reorienting ribs that smashed when he hit the steering wheel. How often must we be told to fasten the seat belt?

His wife came; and this poor lady had no idea that her fine house and elegant style of living depended as much upon nefarious activity as it did upon legitimate enterprise. She had him moved to a private room just along the corridor from where Rosher lay in his annex, where Vennor was reconnected to a supply of blood probably from a vein in a higher social bracket, since she had made of him a private cash-paying patient. They even ran a little couch in, so that she could stay the night if she wanted. And when she remembered that she had left a small leg of pork in the oven with the gas on, they telephoned the police, who sent a man to turn it off. There is a lot to be said for private health care.

Some of these things happened while Inspector Rosher enjoyed yet another nap, and some while he inserted between his formidable brownstone teeth the brown soup, steamed fish with mashed potatoes and cabbage, stewed figs with custard, and strangely flavored tea (probably there is bromide in it, to protect the nurses) which, the British medical profession is persuaded, taken in combination proves efficacious in ninety percent (90%) of cases ranging from scarlet fever to rupture of the spleen. Activity was still going on when the pretty West Indian nurse appeared to take away his empty plates. Well—almost empty, he eschewed the figs. Who needs figs, one leg stuck up in the air?

She said as she picked up the tray, "I'm—sorry—I was rude to you."

"When was that?" he said, with a touch of surprise, because he lived in a world where people are very rude indeed. He hadn't noticed, if she had been. Upset. Defensive. Snappy. People often are, under stress. But not rude, as he understood the term.

"Teatime," she said. "After your friend come in." When she leaned over, driven to plump up his pillows, the curve of her uniformed bosom swelled above his eyes; and the uniformed bosom of a pretty nurse promises softer comfort, somehow, than the naked breasts of your average woman. He was surprised again, by the slight twitch of a libido long dormant. It recoiled from women, in the traumatic time that followed his grope at the publican's wife. He said, "That's all right. Heard a lot worse."

"I was upset."

"Uh-huh. Just thought I might be able to help."

"Nobody can do that, can they? Even if they catch—whoever done it—won't fetch Benjie back, will it?"

"Hm. Bring 'em to book, though, won't it?" Rosher seldom used clichés of this nature. Policemen do not, certainly among themselves. Nail the bastards, they say, or grab 'em by the cobblers. Something like that. But those of the older school tone down for the public, particularly when the public is a gently nurtured young lady. And this one, though black, might well have been gently nurtured. Her voice and manner were gentle. Well—quiet, anyway, and her bosom looked soft.

"Won't bring him back, though, will it?"

"No. It won't bring him back." That's the trouble, with murder. You can't bring 'em back.

She finished the plumping of his pillows, picked up the tray, and went out. Poor little bugger, he thought. Tough on her. And after a while he dozed again. The radio earphones would not fit over his turban, and there seemed to be nothing else to do. Outside his window, darkness fell.

The two young tearaways met no problem on the drive

into town. They passed the scene of the crash, but by now the road was clearer and the vehicles partly screened from them, by darkness and a number of men standing around. So they did not recognize the smashed car. Mike, at the wheel, said, "Some silly bastard's come unstuck."

"Shooden be on the road, half of 'em," said Billy. And because they had more weighty concerns on their minds, and because a man needs to be approaching middle age before he sees another man's misfortune and is sobered—temporarily—by the realization that it could happen to him, they gave the matter no more thought. There were policemen about. They drove on, very circumspectly.

Elton Vennor's garage was on the far side of town, set in an area where the neat and quite clean inhabitants complained to the council from time to time about his scrapyard at the back, bordering on the canal. In justice, they had cause for some complaint when his crane was lugging scrap cars about and his mighty crusher went to work; but this did not happen every day, and never out of working hours. You could not truly call the yard, as some did, an eyesore, because it could not be seen without climbing the ten-foot fence that he agreed to erect all the way around it when the council granted him a lease. He rented it, on a temporary basis; and that site looked better than it did before, when the bulldozers flattened the remains of Buston and Lilywhite, Wholesale Drapers, destroyed by fire, and went away, leaving it all scattered about.

Now the lads approached from the garage side. The frontage is quite impressive, with a showroom for new cars, a good used-car department, an office and reception area built into the big workshops, and six petrol pumps on the concreted forecourt, presided over during open hours by a pensioner who'd gone home long ago.

Nobody seeing a car arrive at this time would note it

as odd. It was still quite early, and at any well-patronized garage cars booked for attention next morning are commonly brought in and left overnight —or in this case, until Monday—by busy men who must be working by the time the mechanics begin to make with the spanners, or to tick the Ministry of Transport list with an oily pencil stub. Here, such cars are driven around to the back of the buildings and left on the concrete fringe of the scrapyard, ignition keys dropped through the workshop letter box.

So the lads followed a well-trodden route, across the forecourt and around to the back; but once out of sight of the front street or, by virtue of that high fence, of anywhere else, they deviated. Billy got out to close and bar the ingress gate, solid like the rest of the fence; while Mike drove on past two vehicles already arrived for tinkering with on Monday, and across the scrap area to the heap of rusted, corroded, scagged, and dented vehicles come at the end to the knacker's yard.

A place was prepared here, cunningly. Jalopies had been propped and set quite artistically, to leave a passage one car wide into and under the stack. Nobody would have noticed it, had they come seeking spare parts as do-it-yourself men do at scrapyards. You can pick up almost anything for a couple of quid, unscrew it yourself. Jalopies fall at all angles, there was nothing queer about this, to the innocent eye.

By the time Billy arrived to help, Mike was down and had his shoulder to the boot. Together they pushed until the souped-up car was nicely hidden, loot and all. It fitted so snugly that no parts-seeking man could get in to examine, let alone cannibalize; and they sealed it in, as instructed, by dragging across the passage entrance—quietly, quietly, no great clanging—a carcass already stripped, and so obviously barren that the gourmet eye would reject it out of hand. This done, they simply walked away.

As they went down the garage-side street, nobody

eyeing them curiously, Billy said, "How about that, then? Piece of bleeding cake."

"All we do now, my son," said Mike, "is count up the bread." And he clutched happily the fat packet in his pocket, found, as promised, taped to the underside of that old, rotten carcass. It did not need counting, there wouldn't be a penny missing. Never had been. But why deny yourself a pleasure?

"We gonna get pissed tonight?" Billy asked.

"We are not," Mike said. "We're going to count it, split it, have a couple of bevvies, and go to bed."

"Fuck that," said Billy. "Let's pick up a couple of birds, get 'em pissed, and how's yer farver. We can afford it."

"Don't talk like a twat. Start flashing it about, people start asking questions, don't they?"

"Tell 'em we flogged a banger, don't we? We done it before."

"No." Don't flash it, Vennor had said. Be sensible, he said, and there'll be plenty more. "We take a few nicker out each, and stash the rest for a Formula One. Right? Or you wanna piss it all away, stick around flogging bangers all your life?"

Billy was grinning again. No great brain, but he knew well enough how to send his friend up. "Only kidding, ain't I? Couple of bevvies and bed. That's what I been fucking saying, ain't it? Don't flash it about, stuff it in your sock. Want a Formula One, don't you?"

And now Mike was grinning. He recognized that his oppo was at it again, and felt no resentment. Never did; and with the elation in him, was not likely to this happy evening. "Watch it, you big, daft bastard," he said, "or I'll put me fucking boot in your cobblers."

"Yeah?" chortled Billy, equally elated and filled with sheer goodwill toward his co-toiler, oppo of his bosom. "You and whose fucking army?"

They walked on, frolicsome. It would have wiped the

smiles off their faces, to have known about Vennor and Nemesis.

All this day, Detective Inspector Young Alec Cruse had been very busy. Detective Chief Superintendent (Percy) Fillimore had not exactly been slouching about; but to Young Alec fell the main legwork and most of the practical organization.

In theory, the inspector on a murder case acts as a sort of filter between the toiling mass below, bringing in snippets gathered by sheer sweat of the feet, and the presiding genius above. All these snippets must be sorted into some kind of order, and presented decently for brooding over. It is the job of the inspector, aided by his sergeant, to handle this aspect of the job, and then to give a hand with the brooding.

This is a tremendous oversimplification, of course. On a big case there will be many inspectors involved, in many departments; many sergeants; and even several superintendents; and to some extent, every job will overlap. In smaller cases, such as the knocking off of a black boy in a dark street, fewer detectives are called upon. The man at the top will almost certainly be juggling with several other capers as big, or even bigger; and so he will leave more to his second-in-command, who must run the whole show, more or less —referring back all the time, of course, to that man who carries the ultimate can. Areas of activity are more clearly defined; but they can cover more ground than the purist would approve.

This is what had happened to Cruse, Percy being engaged with urgent work up to his pointed ears. And the young man did not object; like most policemen, he much preferred active fieldwork to paper. Couldn't dodge all the bumf that accumulates around any murder inquiry; but what he could he delegated, and set off, with relief, to turn a few stones over for himself.

He spent the day mostly in the town center, visiting the pubs, the disco, the drinking clubs; asking questions asked before, in many places, by men from his teams who visited earlier. What tearaways were in last night? What were their names, if known? What did they look like, if not? Were they in gangs, or groups, or did they drink singly? Which way did they go when they left? Tedious work, but necessary. Better than ticking paper at a desk. And his visits to places called upon already should be seen, not as profligate waste of taxpayers' money, but as legitimate follow-up. Very, very often somebody has remembered something by the time the second questioner arrives, mentally jogged by the first caller. Very often somebody will do something silly, like vanishing from where he should be after talking to the first man. The police may—and do—cock up the odd one-off job; but when they doggedly apply an evolved routine, they know what they are doing.

Part of the afternoon he spent at the station, conferring with Percy and the chief constable after a canteen lunch. He used more time in his office, checking reports come in from his team. He went to the hospital, saw the boy's sister, and called upon Rosher. He called on the lad's mother. He returned to the town center, because evening brings the drinkers out again, on Saturday especially, and among them might well be the quarry. A detective cannot afford to ignore the evening, it's when things happen.

So there was his day, and his evening, halfway through which he learned, via his walkie-talkie radio, of an armed raid a few miles away, on the bypass.

Well, it didn't affect him and his work load, he was fully engaged already. But it just goes to show. There's never a letup, is there?

The man who had the most difficult evening was Arnold Gutte. As he rose up in that bus and bopped his head on the parcel rack, there was nothing in his mind but shock. "Mind your nut, chum," the conductor cried. It was too late by then. Through twinkling stars and watery eyes he looked through the window at the crash and thought: *Get out. That's Vennor's car. Is that Vennor, on the stretcher? Oh, my Christ. Get off—find out.*

Then he thought: *No. No—crawling with coppers. And his bloody balaclava'll be in there. Stay clear—you go rushing up asking questions, you can fall right in it.*

It may not be Vennor—on the stretcher—it may be the lorry geezer.

No, it won't. It's the other geezer gets it, not the truckie high up in the cab. Cab's not touched, is it? Look at the bleeding car.

It must be Vennor.

Oh, my Christ.

Sit tight. Stay here. They'll all notice you—they'll all remember you—the conductor'll remember you—if you get off here. And the coppers—there's one right outside the window.

He produced a handkerchief, to wipe streaming eyes. His stocking mask came with it. He palmed it neatly. The old lady in the seat across the gangway cackled gleefully, saying, "Ditten 'arf catch it a crack, ditten you?"

"What? What?" said Arnold.

"I say you ditten 'arf catch it a crack."

"Oh. Yeah." Other people were looking at him, lips curved upward. Nothing renders people so rosy as being allowed to show their gratification when somebody else gets bopped or falls on a banana skin. The old lady's comment united the bus into a sort of conglomerate of pleasure. All this, and a car crash too.

"Daft place to put 'em, I always say," a man in another seat confided in a boozer's baritone. "Ought to have racks at the back, like they do in Israel."

"Can't say I've ever bin there," the old lady said, "but my sister's eldest went to Australia. Doing very well, something to do with sheep. I don't really know all the details, but I know it's sheep."

Nobody was listening; communal attention was back with the crash. The baritone said, "Poor feller on the stretcher—he's lying very still."

"Shooten be surprised if he's dead," the old lady said. Her teeth went nip-nip-nip. "I had a cousin who was. Stands to reason, don't it, flying about in them things?"

Oh, Jesus Christ, thought Arnold Gutte. What a fucking turnup.

He stayed with the bus all the way into town, alighting at his intended stop well away from home. His car waited nearby. The old lady beamed and nodded encouragingly as he passed, saying, "I go on to the depot."

He fretted his way to the side street where he had left his car. Moving on from shock, his mind realized fully the state things were in, if what he was sure had happened had indeed happened, and knocked out Elton Vennor. Because nobody else would have any kind of overall knowledge about the job. All anybody knew was the limited action they themselves had taken. Nobody knew what was supposed to happen next, or in the near future.

This was Vennor's policy. Everything played very close to the chest. What a feller doesn't know, he said, he can't spill if he gets picked up, or liquored up, or shacked up with an inquisitive and prattling popsy. Everybody accepted it, it was one of the things that won him respect. And it is, in truth, a wise policy—so long as the man with his fingers on all the buttons keeps his health.

Vennor, by the look of it, had lost his. Temporarily, or permanently by dying, made very little difference, so far as the job was concerned. The thing was: if anybody knew how things stood now, it was not Arnold; and if it wasn't Arnold, it was nobody. He was, always, Vennor's trusted lieutenant. Trusted, that is, so far as Vennor trusted anybody.

I don't even know, the man thought now as he drove home, *where those two herberts are taking the jalopy. The garage? I don't know. Seems the obvious place. I imagine the Vauxhall he was driving was supposed to go there. Didn't tell me, did he? And his bloody balaclava'll still be in it.*

They'll take it to the bleeding police pound.

They're going to find out it was knocked, ain't they? So if they tumble him—are they going to be straight onto us?

Now, don't bleeding panic. It don't necessarily follow. I mean, he won't keep no written records. Not with names on 'em, he's not a bleeding idiot. Or he wasn't.

I'd better have a look at the garage.

No. No. The Old Bill could be there. With the jalopy. Maybe the other fellers. And the two herberts.

Stay clear. Ring the others, when you get home.

Yes—I know you're not supposed to make contact. But it's a bleeding emergency, ain't it?

But sod it—you don't even have a phone number for the herberts, do you? So how do you get in touch with them? You don't know where they live, you don't know their names—nothing. And they'll be the only ones who know where the tickle went.

He lived in a decent little house, one of a whole road of decent little houses, all identical. He kept a little wife in his, of whom he was rather fond so long as she kept her station. When he entered, she said, "Hallo, dear. Supper in ten minutes, it's shepherd's pie."

Shepherd's pie? At a time like this? "I may have to go out again," he said, making for the telephone.

"Oh," she said. "I do wish you'd told me, dear, I'd have done a salad." Salad you can keep fresh, under a sheet of plastic wrap; but shepherd's pie deteriorates, no doubt about that. It's horrible, warmed up.

"Something's come up," he told her, dialing.

She could see that. It did not unduly worry her. Something often did. Unlike Mrs. Vennor, she knew her husband was bent, and the wives of the bent get quite used to watching them chew their fingernails. She did not know what he was up to—never did—but if he was about to depart again for one of his very rare spells of porridge—well, one could quite look forward to it, really. It was rather nice, having the house all to herself; and he was a good provider, he never left her lacking for money. If there was a drawback attached to being married to him, apart from the normal rubs of marriage itself, it was being called Mrs. Gutte. So she went quietly away into the lounge (all these houses have a lounge), closing the door behind her. He did not like to be listened to when he made telephone calls. And the less she knew, the less she could tell. She liked it that way.

He tried Joe "Plonker" Milgrave's number first. They called him Plonker because of the way he played the piano. The phone rang out for a long time. Joe still lived with his mother and father, a thirty-five-year-old cuckoo who knew when he was well off. They must have been out. He must have been out.

He'd been driving the other car. Should have transferred the shotguns and the men from the Smoke to the third car in a convenient lay-by, and gone on to plant the Rover in the big city.

Surely, oh surely, he hadn't piled up?

Before or after the transfer? There were masks and offensive weapons in that car, if he did it before.

The old folks hadn't been called out to the hospital. Had they?

Now, don't panic, don't panic, Arnold said to himself; and he rang Cauliflower Davis, so called because of his ear.

The Cauliflower answered in person. " 'Ello," he said.

"Collie?" said Arnold. Cauliflower is a cumbersome mouthful. They called him Collie for short. "Listen— it's Arnold."

"What are you doing on the bleeding blower?" Alarm sounded in Collie's voice. One sensed that he was about to sever the connection.

"Don't hang up, don't hang up," Arnold cried, urgently. "Listen—the boss has hit a lorry."

"Hit a lorry?"

"In the Vauxhall. On the way back to town."

"Oo fuck," said Collie.

"Where's Plonker, I can't get Plonker."

"City. Took the Rover, didden he?"

"Yeah, but he ought to be back by now. Didn't he?"

Or did he? Arnold didn't really know. It would take a little time, obviously, to dump the stolen car in the big city. How was he coming back, by train? Made sense, to plant the car there, preferably by the railway station or somewhere like it. Any place suggesting the getaway went on from there. Draw pursuit away, trail a little aniseed. Vennor was no twat, he knew what he was doing. Snag was, nobody else did. "Listen," Arnold said. "The Squashed Hedgehog. Right away."

"Yeah. Yeah," said Collie, and put the phone down.

The Squashed Hedgehog was a roadhouse newly built on the main road, the far side of town from where Vennor's accident happened. Named by a proprietor with a sardonic bent for one of the main features of modern Britain's highways and leafy byways. The name proved to be quite an attraction. It amused people. They fell about, when they first heard it. Specialty of the barman was the Squashed Hedgehog cocktail, the color of blood and containing shreds of melon. The melon was put through a mincer, to make it look like meat. Clever, that.

Arnold and Collie drove into the concrete car park almost at the same time, so that they walked together into the great, glass-shimmering pile of breeze block crisscrossed with plastic beams. It even had plastic-framed Georgian bay windows. They went into a plastic bar, one of two so similar that many a man, getting assiduously stoned in one, left it for the lavatory and came back to complete the stoning, wondering where his friends had gone.

When they were seated on bright plastic seats at an inadequate but private plastic table, Arnold told everything he knew.

Collie said, "Dead, is he?"

"I don't know." They were speaking in whispers. Near-whispers, anyway. "He could have been, he wasn't moving."

"Fucking hooray," said Collie.

"Where do the herberts hang out?" Arnold asked. "The two lads."

"I don't know, do I? Don't know nothing about 'em, they was Mr. Vennor's choosing." Notice the prefix? Mark of respect. "Don't even know their names, do I?"

No, you wouldn't, Arnold thought. If he didn't tell me, he wouldn't tell you. He said, "Nor do I. What do you reckon we ought to do?"

"We oughta find out about Mr. Vennor. Maybe he only got bumped a bit, maybe he's all right. We oughta give the hospital a bell."

Of course. A man may lie prone and without moving in a boxing ring, given the incentive of a belt on the button. Carried away on a stretcher, one could well think him dead if that were one's only glimpse of him. I've been, Arnold told himself, going off half-cocked. He pulled coins from his pocket and sorted through them. Said to Collie, "Got any ten p's? I'll ring 'em from here."

He used the phone booth provided as one of the roadhouse amenities. Yes, said the hospital, when it had eaten up two of his tenpenny pieces while it checked. Yes, they had Mr. Vennor here, he had just been moved to a private room. No, they were not encouraging visitors just at this moment, because Mr. Vennor was still unconscious. No, they did not know as yet how serious Mr. Vennor's injuries were, Dr. Lovejoy was still with him. Was he a relative?

"Er—no," said Arnold. "Just good friends."

"Ah," said the hospital. "Perhaps you would like to try again in the morning." And it hung up.

Arnold went back to the table. "He's still out," he said. "They've got him in a private room."

"Ain't dead, then," said Collie. "Is he?"

"Must have got himself bashed about, though. No visitors, they reckon."

"I think we oughta go over there. He might be conscious, time we get there."

"*I* think," Arnold said, "we ought to go back to that barn. The lads won't have left yet, they'll be there till after dark."

"Fuck that. It'll *be* dark, time we arrive. There'll be fuzz on the bypass, won't there? And more on the main road, if they haven't cleared the crash away. And what you going to do, if we get hold of the herberts? If they ain't there, we haven't done nothing, have we? Might as well sit here. We don't know where Mr. Vennor's told 'em to stash the jalopy, do we? So we run them coppers all for nothing. And if we catch 'em—well, I ain't driving around with that jalopy, not with all that fuzz about. Not with my form. Are you? They'll have roadblocks up."

"There might be fuzz at the hospital."

"Ah. Aye. Well—sod it. I reckon we oughta go anyway. Find out where he is, even if we can't see him. Any fuzz handy, we don't have to hang about, do we? Don't have to go near, soon's we spot 'em we peel off into a ward, or something. We're visiting somebody else."

Arnold ruminated. Said, "Bit bloody chancy, ain't it?"

"So's sitting on our arses. Ain't it?" Collie looked as if he might at any moment begin to crack his knuckles.

Not a habit to which he was prone, but stress does strange things to people. Arnold, for instance, was twitching at the corner of the mouth. He said, "Yeah —but they might have searched the Vauxhall, found his balaclava. They might be waiting to question him."

"They won't bugger his car about just because he's been in an accident. Private property, ain't it? They just run 'em into the pound."

"You never know what the bastards'll do, do you?"

"You got a better idea?"

"Yeah. Scarper."

"With the Old Bill just got a snatch in? Move out now, you're right in the shit, you and your bleeding driving record. And all them bleeding roadblocks."

As it happens, there were no roadblocks; but shocked imagination pictured them everywhere.

"Lie low, then. Stay home. Vennor won't keep records, will he?"

"Listen—Mr. Vennor comes out of that hospital, finds you let all that gelt go—he ain't gonna be very happy, is he? Nor's anyone. Like them geezers in the Smoke. Nobody's gonna like losing that sort of bread, are they? It's all up to you, really."

"Why me?"

"You're like second-in-command, ain't you? Like in the army. The leader gets shot, the second-in-command takes over."

"How can I take over? I don't know nothing—"

"That's why we have to get to Mr. Vennor. Find out. Then we'll all know where we stand."

"I'll go—tomorrow." Or I'll have scarpered. "He's unconscious—"

"Tonight. You'll have to go tonight. Find out what the form is. He might be conscious by now. You gotta get in fast." Before, Collie meant, the fuzz had itself thoroughly organized.

The bent have, by necessity, a good working knowledge of the law. The police can inspect but they cannot search a private car, without suspicion attached to it. Unless by unhappy accident, provided Vennor had stuffed it under a seat cushion or in the glove compartment like a cleaning rag, they would not have found that balaclava. Not yet, anyway, with the smashed vehicle only just cleared from the road. But tomorrow . . . Never mind the bloody law—who can say, with the fuzz, what will have been done by tomorrow?

So it was Collie who put his friend Arnold over the barrel. And Arnold knew it, even as they talked. He was, it must be remembered, a crook of good repute among his fellow bent. He could hardly walk away whistling from a job with a fortune in it, there are standards to be maintained, there are ethics. More people than those directly involved—and villains deprived of such a cut can turn very nasty—would look askance. Rough people who had worked with Mr. Vennor before, and hoped to do so again.

Quite apart from probable physical violence committed at some future date on him, the bastard who chickened, and having to wave farewell to his own share of this rich tickle and the ease and comfort it would bring for a considerable part of the rest of his life, it was a matter of face. Lose that and you lose all. And maybe your looks or that life with it, if the cognoscenti take it very hard.

He sat for a time in silence, while all this and more came home to him. Like: Vennor would certainly have his guts, if he came out and found Arnold had let the side down. Or worse: if he faced trial, the jalopy discovered because it had been left where the lads stashed it, and brought home to him. Sod it—they'd all face trial. Curtains for Arnold. No way out—he must, as Collie had pointed out, assume the mantle of command. It was forced upon him. He said at last, "Yeah. All right, I'll go up there. You'd better get into town, see if you can get hold of them lads."

"Soon as I've seen you safely through the gates," said Collie. "I'll drive behind you."

Yes, you little bastard, Arnold thought as they left the roadhouse, two small men lost without a leader: *you mean to see I do it, don't you? I said too much. You don't trust me, you think I might scarper.* He thought it without surprise. Whoever coined the cliché concerning honor among thieves didn't know what the hell he was talking about. With this kind of tickle at stake?

In another thing Collie was right. It would have been dark by the time they got back to the barn. Arnold turned in at the hospital gate, seeing in his rearview mirror the following car drive on along the road, at just about the time when the two lads were preparing to leave the barn, Inspector Rosher asked Nurse Holness for a bottle, and a man in London called Gentleman Jack Hagger decided that something, definitely, had gone wrong. Arnold steered into the car park area, a wary eye rolling around. No coppers here. If there were any, they'd be inside.

When he entered the bright and clack-floored reception hall, he said to the girl at the desk, "You—er—have you got my friend in here? A Mr. Vennor."

The girl studied a list. She was in her first week on this job, and not yet fully controlling it. She said, "Mr. Vennor is on the first floor, in the Ferguson Room. But I don't think—" (Wards here are commonly named after local worthies, who bequeathed money to the hospital rather than have it fall into the cackling clutch of relatives.)

"Thank you," said Arnold, and he turned to the stairs.

"Come back," the girl cried. But the telephone rang, an emergency call; and here came that young, good-looking doctor who appeared very frequently to pass the time of day and boldly eye her bristols; and a girl cannot attend to everything at once. Quite made her blush, he did.

There is a sign at the top of the stairs, telling the curious that to the right is the Beeson Ward, and to the left, beyond Fanny Buckett Ward (what a woman she was: three times mayor and an Olympic bronze for shot-putting), the Ferguson Room. Straight on for Orthopedic. Arnold, after a squint from the corner of his eye, turned left. Still no sign of policemen.

He approached the Ferguson Room—no identification problem, each door had a label above it—passing first the entrance to Fanny Buckett Ward and then the door to the annex. Wherein lay Inspector Rosher, who, in spite of the fact that his door stood open, did not see him go by because he was frowning up at the ceiling.

As Arnold came close to the door he wanted, it opened, and a tall starched woman came out. She said, "Can I help you? I'm the Sister."

"Ah," said Arnold. "Yes. Thank you. I'm visiting Mr. Vennor."

"No visitors, I'm afraid. Are you a relative?"

"No." And then, realizing that being related conferred some kind of edge, "Well—a sort of—in-law."

"Mr. Vennor is still unconscious, unfortunately. Mrs. Vennor is with him, but I'm afraid she's very upset. Who shall I say called?"

"Ah. Yes. It doesn't matter. Thank you." He turned and walked swiftly away. Sister went into her office, which is on the other side of the corridor.

Inspector Rosher, eyes down now from the ceiling, saw him go by this time. He thought: that's Arnold Gutte. In a hurry. What's he doing here?

5

Up in the Big Smoke, in a very luxurious apartment on the edge of wicked Soho, the man Hagger, called Gentlemen Jack, was at this very moment tying his black bow before turning to don the dinner jacket held for him by a blue-chinned gentleman's gentleman with a discreet automatic holstered under his armpit. Hagger was saying to a second penguin-appareled man sitting easy in an easy chair, "I think we can take it that something has gone wrong."

"Unless dis Vennor geezer's werkin' a flanker," the other man said.

"He'd be very unwise to try it," said Hagger. This was the man who put the bent guard in that security van, his were the shock troops currently on the way back to London. And what a contrast in accents here: his own urbane, soft-tongued, with a hint almost of Upper Crust, which he definitely was not; the other, in tone and timbre, ideally suited to crying fish from a barrow.

"So dey're all de same, dese little provincial geezers, ayn' dey? Fink dey can put one over, doan dey? Remember Leeds? 'Adder go up and break 'is bleetin' legs, ditten we? Why ayn' 'e rung?"

"If something's gone up the stick, presumably he

couldn't. And still can't. Thank you, Charles." The last he addressed to the gentleman's gentleman, who had handed him a silk handkerchief, ready folded. He arranged it fastidiously in his breast pocket. Handcrafted, the suit. No rubbish, you could feel the quality.

"Bunny rang in, ditten 'e? So de job wen' all right." Bunny was the guard. He was in the car now, traveling up. It had stopped while he reported, per order, that Uncle was doing well. Elton Vennor should have rung in, too. That was the arrangement. But he hadn't.

"If I were working a flanker," said Jack Hagger, "I should ring in *before* I scarpered. Why arouse suspicion? One little call, and you get at least a day or two start, don't you? If nobody is expecting to hear from you again until then." By nobody, he meant himself.

"Yeah, well," the other man said. His chin was as blue as the chin of the gentleman's gentleman and almost as rugged; and if his suit did not bulge beneath the armpit, it could have been because the very good barathea had been cut to accommodate. "Yeah, well. Doan nececelery fink of fings like dat, do dey, bleetin' provincials? Aht of dere bleetin' league, ayn' dey?"

"I had this Vennor well checked. He seems to be an intelligent operator."

"Well, den—why ayn' 'e bin on de blower?"

"That, Georgie, is the question." Hagger was ready to go, very elegant. A man is really at his best, if he has one, at around forty. Georgie got up from his chair. Not every man matures to handsome, but his tailor had worked on it. Not much can be done with a figure that is almost square. The elegant man addressed his personal gentleman. "If any calls come, Charles, I want them straight away. At the Consul Club."

"Ain't I coming with you, then?" The gentleman's gentleman spoke almost aggressively. He took the bodyguarding part of his work very seriously. Not wanted, he felt it as a slight.

Hagger spoke quite gently. Another good leader,

who understood his men. "I need you here, somebody reliable has to stand by the phone. If no call comes, you'll be traveling with us tomorrow. Give it a couple of hours, then pack a few shirts. We'll go and see for ourselves, find out what's going on." Notice how coolly the really big operator reacts, even when all that money is dotted, suddenly, with a question mark.

"Dat's de ticket," said Georgie. "Gee da bastards up a bit."

Detective Inspector Rosher had been frowning at the ceiling when Arnold went by mainly to ease the neck muscles. He had nothing more interesting to look at, anyway. The coffee-skinned nurse was not present, and he was no reader. Never had been. She had brought in some paperback books, because most people read in the hospital; but they were all detective novels, except one that dealt with the love feast of a Nurse Felicity Brownlowe who was swept off her feet by a handsome sheikh in a desert; and detective novels, he knew, are a load of old cobblers. As are stories about Nurse Felicity Brownlowe. You can tell by the covers.

The fact is, he was bored. Active men with small inner resources inevitably are, confined to bed, even at home with loved ones to bedevil. Rosher had no loved ones. Except for his work and boxing, he had no real interests; and only the completely besotted can lie forever wondering what are the chances of Harry Doakes if he ever goes in with the world champion, as he is clamoring to do.

Life is full of irony, isn't it? A man with a hundred things demanding thought—a working policeman, say, in this wicked age—is kept so busy as new matter adds to the demand that he has very little chance to do it properly, all on his own and uninterrupted. When he has all the time in the long day and a measure of privacy, too—as in hospitals—he finds he has nothing to think about. Oh, Rosher had run all his outstanding cases through his mind; but he knew most of the answers already, and other people were clearing them now. All he found in them was mental pabulum. No solid nourishment.

So the soil of his mind was tilled and ready for seeding when Arnold Gutte hurried suddenly past, just as the head came down. That's Arnold Gutte, he thought. In a hurry. What's he doing here?"

He lay awhile thinking, having at last something, however small, for the brain to set against sterilized boredom. Under the white turban his jutting brows drew down above little eyes which took on the glossy, almost ferocious look that came upon them when he was mentally engaged. He really did astonishingly resemble a gorilla, dressed up and dumped in bed for a mad commerical. And resenting it. When Nurse Holness came in she started at the sight of him, quite visibly. "Are you all right?" she said.

He replied with a question. "Who's along the corridor?"

"Lot of people, if you mean the Fanny Buckett Ward." Among the staff it was known as the Fuckett Ward, but she wasn't telling him that.

"No—the other way. That way." He pointed.

"Oh. Well—Sister," she said. "In her office."

Sister? Why would the little bastard visit Sister? Well, he might, you never knew. He'd been visiting somebody, you don't just choose a hospital to trot up and down the corridors of for exercise. "Are there any more wards along there?"

"No wards. The Ferguson Room, that's private. We got a man in there, unconscious. Car crash, brought in while you was having a nap."

"What's his name?"

"I don't know, I didn't ask. Why?" She added—not very sensibly, but the police and her brother were obviously intermingled at present in her mind, "Nothing to do with Benjie, is it?"

"Benjie?"

"My brother. Or don't you bother to remember?"

"Ah. Yes—yes, of course. No. Well—no." Nothing to do with Benjie. Nothing to do with anything, really. Just the antenna twitching around. Just the wide-nostriled nose with the hairs in it, sniffing. "No. I just wondered. Can you find out?"

"Sure. No problem, I'll know in no time anyway. Now let's tuck you in a little." And again that soft-seeming bosom came down to within inches of his quickly refocused eyes. Again he felt the twitch of surprised libido as he said, "What for?"

"Time to bed you down for the night."

"Already?"

"Yep. We like to get you off early so we can wake you up in the small hours, give you a sleeping pill."

The bosom moved. Pillows plumped all over again, she began to tuck in the blankets. In his mind's eye he saw suddenly the soft brown breasts, nippled under her rustling uniform. Enough of that! He said, "How long am I going to be here?"

"That's up to Doctor. He'll want to be sure your head's all right."

"Nothing wrong with my head."

"How do you know? Might fall to pieces when we take the bandages off."

In spite of himself his lips curled upward, showing a glimmer of big brown incisors. Her answering smile was a wide, white grin, clearing completely for a while the lingering sadness and whatever hurt she had felt at his failing to remember her brother's name. Good teeth she had, showed up well in her brown face. He asked, because Sister might be the little sod Gutte's sister, or something, "What's Sister's name?"

"Ward. Ward Sister Ward. Can't all be lucky, can we? There—that ought to hold you. Sleep tight." She rustled from the room.

Got sand, that one, he thought. Guts. No weeping

and wailing. Not in public. Settling his aching shoulders in the sterile bed, pottery leg hung still in its sling, he felt warm liking for her. Courage was a quality he understood and respected.

He could not sleep. Few people do during the first few nights in a hospital, especially with a limb slung up and aching. The involuntary naps that come by day when nature tries to compensate don't help, either. He'd been in before, he knew the pattern and cursed it. He was a man who knew how to curse. She came again later, saying, "Do you want a sleeping pill?"

"No," he said. Bugger drugs, he'd shunned them all his life. "Do you work all the time?"

"Shifts. Roll on changeover day."

"I mean, are you busy now?" He had not been thinking of the hours she labored. CID men themselves work long and very odd hours, they are well used to seeing the same faces at any time of the day or night.

"Not really. If you don't count me crossword."

"Well—why don't we have a bit of a chat?" It came from him with gruff awkwardness. Not an invitation Old Blubbergut was used to making. Perhaps sheer boredom and the fret of not sleeping edged him into it. Perhaps that inner vision of her breasts had something to do with it. Maybe it was simply because she was warm, and very likable, and her brother had been murdered. Probably it was a mix of all three. He added, "Pass the time away. Hrrmph."

"Why not?" she said. "There's a lot of it about."

She stayed almost half an hour. Then she went away to tend a fretful patient; and looking in afterward, finding him still awake, she stayed another half-hour.

By the end of that time—he was surprised by the mental ease between them, and willing to admit that it must be coming from her; she did not tighten up, as people usually did in his grim presence—he knew that she spent her early years in Port of Spain, Jamaica. Her father came over first, sent for her mother and herself when he settled, bus conducting. Her brother was born here. No trouble—didn't even smoke, hardly touched liquor, because his dear ambition was to play cricket for the county and for England. Or for the West Indies, he didn't really mind which. Her father died.

And she learned a little, too, because she asked if he didn't have a wife, children, relatives, friends; because nobody but colleagues had come to visit him. He was divorced, he said. Lived alone in his house on the hill. No children. No relatives. Friends? Well—not much time for them, really. He worked peculiar hours.

"Well," she said at last, "can't sit here all night. Shouldn't have sat here at all, Sister'd raise hell, only she's in her office with some stomach mixture." And at the door she turned to ask, with difficulty—it was the first crack he had seen in her brave façade, "Do you think you'll—get—whoever—did it to Benjie?"

Poor little bugger, he thought. "I don't see why not. We usually do."

She was a nice girl. Nice figure, too. But sod that, he'd had enough of that. Besides, she was out of his age group.

He slept, when she was gone.

6

The newspapers next morning did not splash the robbery across the front pages. The local rag would have done, and did the day after; but the local rag does not publish on Sunday. This was Sunday, and Sunday papers have sex on their minds and are too preoccupied with color supplements to bother much with any news that does not feature Gay Vicar and Mother of Five or how to create your own wine cellar out of an abandoned egg crate. Justice to them: viewed nationally, it was small beer as a story.

These national papers, then, if they mentioned the matter at all, tossed it into the clutter of inside pages. It seemed, after all, just one such caper among many. But it was, in fact, much bigger than it looked, and the story had a second level that certainly would have interested them more.

If they went further than a bald sentence stating that a robbery had been attempted—not carried out, just been attempted; Vennor's plan went beautifully— it was merely to mention that the cargo aboard the security van had been left untouched. Police believed, the reporters said, that the robbers panicked for some reason (one put it down to swift action by the guards in the escorting car), and lifting up their skirts, they'd scarpered. Only two bothered to report that the guard riding inside the van was missing; possibly kidnapped inadvertently, possibly a plant who'd legged it with the rest.

Even the police had no idea of the true facts. But then, this is often the case.

The chief constable, Detective Chief Superintendent (Percy) Fillimore (who received the case on top of the black boy's murder and his normal top-heavy work load), and all the policemen in town and the big city who were called upon to scrutinize the matter certainly believed that the guard was a plant, such plantings being commonplace to the point of tedium; but they were astray in thinking that the tickle in the van was left there because the villains panicked.

Small blame to them. Many a job blows up after months of meticulous planning—people even get shot—because some overimaginative operator suddenly cracks, and spreads panic and confusion among his cohorts. That's when the guns go bang, that's when the tires shriek. That's when the little man who broke finds himself shortly blowing bubbles from a riverbed with concrete all over his feet.

Here are the facts.

There was in the big city a highly respected and respectable jeweler. A mild little man with a meek and ready smile that showed all his expensive teeth as far around as the molars. He had two other shops in London, quite big ones; and he was a fence on a very considerable scale. So:

A good deal of legitimate merchandise passed among these three shops. Gold and silver baubles, consignments of rings and things, various high-priced artifacts; and he sent them by security van, hired often and often over the years. The security firm doesn't know it to this day, but it has carried a king's ransom in stolen goodies, hidden very craftily among these legitimate loads of wife sweetener and crumpet bait. The jeweler is—or was (he will have lost faith in the system by now)—on hand to receive them at whichever end they arrived. The jeweler himself unpacked them.

Now: there was a heist in Germany (you'll have read about that in the papers), more than two million pounds' worth—not marks, mind you; pounds sterling—of variegated twinkle, hijacked en route from one town of an exhibition tour to another. The story got a lot of coverage even in England, about two years ago. By international wheeling (jewelers have legitimate contacts in the continental diamond centers and so on) certain dealing took place, and all that twinkle came in by light aircraft to a dark English field on a dark English night, and wound up in the vault of this jeweler. In a big city, but not in London. The world's capitals were being combed; but you can't comb every town in the world.

It stayed there two whole years, while the heat cooled a little and the jeweler gloated many nights alone in his vault. He was in no hurry to get rid of the stuff. Even on the undercover market good jewels appreciate in value all the time.

But jewelry stores on the retail side do not. He began to feel the pinch, having invested a fortune to get the things. His big city branch was losing money, and as a good—and, incidentally, very rich—businessman he could not abide an unprofitable lurk. So he decided to pare down. The heat had cooled. Transfer everything from here to London. Keep the pawnbroking side open—pawnbrokers flourish in recessions—and take the small shop next door to it, stocked with a few trays of rings, watches, and trinkets. This, to maintain his toehold in the trade that allowed him to keep a profitable vault. This business is still there, perhaps you pass it every day.

Most of his stock, then, was gone: several security-truck loads, all transported without incident. He packed the tickle in the last lot and took himself off to

London, where he had a buyer all lined up, ready to pay from a suitcase and with a route open all the way to America. The security firm raised no eyebrows at his choosing Saturday afternoon for the run. It made sense, and it's been done before. By the time the truck reached London his store would be closed. Offloading could be done without disturbing the flow of business, and he would have all Sunday to check legitimate lists and rearrange storing and display.

What he did not know was: he nurtured a viper in his bosom. A manager who had worked for him three years, and was married to Vennor's sister. Who was straight as a die, whatever that may be. She'd actually reformed the man.

Because he, too, had once been a naughty lad. Had his own business, did fencing under cover of it just as his current boss did. Handled a lot of stuff for Vennor— and for Gentleman Jack Hagger in the days before Hagger battled his way up the ladder. Simple burglar Hagger was then, and Vennor working hard to consolidate both facets of his business.

Well: through dealings with her brother he met Vennor's sister, and he married her; and got himself caught. Three years, Strangeways. When he came out he had a son two years old (unpurse the lips, he got full remission) and a wife who had waited faithfully. He put her in the family way again immediately, on the couch almost as he walked in through the door. He then adjusted his dress, and went straight.

Almost straight. Little matters like forged references and back history had to be manipulated; but many a man has done that, and thereafter lived a blameless life.

Alas, the leopard cannot wholly desert his spots. Sensitive antenna and a vault never visited except by the boss himself tell a man the boss is bent, and this in a trade of which he himself knows all the twists. And if he has patience he will have access, at some time, to the boss's keys. All he needs is a couple of minutes with them and a piece of silly putty. In this case a substance called Bluetack, useful in the shop for attaching things to walls and windows and guaranteed not to mark. If the vault has a combination lock, and he lacks skill with the tumblers, there is a little computerized gadget now so simple . . . But enough of this, Lead us not into temptation.

The bone of the matter is: there are police and trade sheets that circulate to jewelers all over the world, listing and often illustrating stolen properties. He managed a peek at what was in that vault. The mounts were gone, melted down long ago; but one glorious ring had been left untouched. Presumably, whoever ordered the melting felt that it was too beautiful to spoil, and the jeweler agreed. After all, it added nothing to the bulk. In a state of almost unbelieving excitement, because this was opportunity knocking with a vengeance, he got in touch with Vennor and, that man saying he would need outside help, with Jack Hagger.

Not difficult, given so shrewd a worker on the inside, to know when to attack. For sure, if the boss man did not go to London to receive the gear when it arrived, the gear was not with the load. And easy to check every night, when you live above the shop, to see what is gone from the vault. When the boss announces on Saturday that he will be going to London, you make a couple of phone calls.

Simple. And the raid went so smoothly. So now the car stood hidden in Elton Vennor's scrapyard; with no Elton Vennor there to do the strictly private things he had meant to do to it, all on his own over the weekend.

7

Sunday in the town is a quiet day, after the dawn-wandering drunks go home or are locked away. Sunday anywhere in Britain is a quiet day, their Puritan God being a sour-faced old bastard with whiskers who elevates aweful eyebrows at levity on the Sabbath, and usually makes it rain. Today He held back. Made it chilly, with a nasty wind out of the east. Gray sky, with precipitation as a petty-minded threat. It was occurring, off Ronaldsway.

At just about the time when those who fear Him emerged from His dry-rot-and-old-hassock-perfumed temples, Elton Vennor was rushed from the Ferguson Room into the Intensive Care Unit. Sudden deterioration. Heart attack: caused by the shock of the accident, the doctors said, aggravated by the stoving in of ribs. While two Pakistani nurses resheeted the vacated bed, two unspectacular cars were arriving in town, both borrowed last night, from curbsides in London. By friends of Gentleman Jack Hagger, who drove one with his gentleman's gentleman seated beside him. In the other was Georgie Burtin, a man of simple tastes—he liked, simply, money and violence and a woman from time to time—and long-term lieutenant to this highly dangerous leader in whose service he enjoyed a great deal of all three. Free ride, for the latter. Hagger had brothels among his many interests.

They arrived in the town market square, called quaint by many, with no definite course of action in mind. How could they have? How, that is, could Hagger have? The others would do as they were told when he had performed the necessary thinking, based on whatever he found here. If all was well—no sweat. Back to the Smoke, with a pleasant lunch on the way. If all was not . . .

Your good leader keeps a balanced view. The guard Bunny, arrived home, had reported that the raid went beautifully. Good. That was as it should be. And Vennor's not ringing—well, it was not necessarily a pointer to evil, the gear in a holdall and a quick scarper. Notoriously, you can try any given phone number any given number of times, and never connect. Not once.

This he pointed out to Georgie as they sat in the bar of the Black Bull, which had just opened its doors. Georgie, as second-in-command, had no need for the balanced view. On the contrary, one of his great attributes was his quick suspicion cogently expressed, his constant watching of his own and his leader's back. He said, "He coulda got on to de operator, told 'er 'e was 'aving trouble. I've done it meself."

"Uh-huh," said Jack Hagger. "He could have. It means giving the number, though, doesn't it? Operators remember things like that, people ringing London from hick towns. And they listen in, sometimes. So she'd have had his number and mine, all written down on her little pad. Or whatever."

"Coulda sent a telegram." This was Charles, the gentleman's gentleman.

"Same thing, isn't it? All written down." More ineradicably than if you phone through the operator, he did not trouble to point out. Telegram forms are filed. Well, they were good boys. They did their best.

"Wojjer gonna do, den?" asked Georgie, knowing full well.

"Call on Vennor. Drink up."

They came out from the Black Bull and Georgie eyed the town square, which gives aesthetic satisfaction to so many. "Wadda bleetin' dump," he said, with the contempt of the Londoner gone beyond Watford. "Where's dis geezer live?"

"See the post office over there?" said Jack Hagger. "That's a phone box outside it. There'll be a local directory in it. Charles—take this ball-point. Go and find his address."

"Haven't got no paper," the gentleman's gentleman said.

"Tear a bit off the directory." Patience, patience. Marvelous man in a brawl. "And look under *V*."

No problem, finding Vennor in the book. Charles came back with his address written down, in heavy-breathing capitals on a scrap of torn paper. Anybody looking for Vanter, E. J., or Vanwick, P. N., would be out of luck, their listing drove off in a motor car. Couldn't have rung them from there, anyway, if it's any consolation. The booth had been vandalized. Georgie came into Hagger's car for the short drive to leafy Deacon Avenue, where Vennor's home stood nicely centered in its own grounds. One car calling is less obtrusive than two, and there is no restriction on Sunday parking in the square. The one left there would be safe enough, both cars wore false plates and had been cleverly tarted up with quick-dry enamel. Easy, when you have contacts everywhere.

They found, of course, nobody at home. Mrs. Vennor was at the hospital, and the only living-in servant, a middle-aged cook-cum-housemaid called Elsie Freemantle, had gone as usual to the Mount of Zion, where she prayed for Mr. Vennor in a brown tweed coat and a varnished straw hat with cherries on.

"Wadda we do now, den?" said Georgie, as they

reunited back on the handsome porched front step after a separated prowl around each side of the house, peering in through the windows.

A question not easy to answer, right off the cuff. Hagger said, "I think we'd better ask at the house next door. See if they know what time he left." Was he carrying a suitcase, did he go by car or call a cab. Was his wife with him, if he had one. Or his mistress, if he had not. Or both, if all were kinky.

"Bet 'e ditten come back," said Georgie. "Bet 'e wen' aht on de job, and scarpered straight orf."

It happened that they had no need to call at the house next door, which stood, as Vennor's did, in its own miniature park. As they drove out from the drive the next-door lady came legging it in at the gate. A Mrs. Froggett, dressed in a floral bell tent, smiling an eager smile and waving a beringed and podgy hand, the swag beneath her chin woggling with the vigor of her oncoming. Mr. Froggett is a well-known master butcher, and they eat very well. She cried as she came, "I say! I say!"

Jack Hagger reined the car in and wound the window down. The lady loomed alongside, crying through her rosebud beam, "Were you looking for Mr. and Mrs. Vennor?"

"Yes, madam," said Gentleman Jack.

The beam grew wider; and yet into the core of it she managed to inject a flavor of dolor. "He's been hurt, I'm afraid."

"Hurt?"

"He crashed in his car. In the hospital. I understand he's not allowed visitors. Mrs. Vennor is with him, poor thing. And the maid will be at the chapel."

Nicely encapsulated. Right in a nutshell. "Ah," said Hagger. "Ah."

"Can I give him a message or anything?" the eager lady cried.

"Er—no. Which—er—hospital would he be in?"

"St. Barnolph's, we only have the one."

"And where is St. Barnolph's?" Jack Hagger was rightly nicknamed. He was the perfect gentleman—when it suited him.

"On the Hutton Fellowes road. Just beyond the first roundabout, you can't miss it. But I don't think you can see him. He's in the Ferguson Room."

"Thank you very much, dear." He began to wind the window up.

"Who shall I say called?" The lady stood with her head cocked, like a fat and eager, well-intentioned hen.

"Just friends." Hagger made his own not unattractive smile and set the car moving again. The lady thought what a nice man, and started back to her house. Long time since anybody called her dear.

"Whadda we do now?" asked Georgie.

"Take a look at this hospital."

Other things were happening all over the town. That goes without saying. To concentrate on two: the tearaway Billy Purvis was sniffing glue. And the man they called the Cauliflower (Collie for short) was about to point his motor car at that same St. Barnolph's hospital, talked into it by Ratface Denny Rorke, Joe "Plonker" Milgrave, and Arnold Gutte.

They held a meeting this morning. They'd held one the previous night, when Plonker got back from losing the Rover in the city, but that was very scrappy, everybody too shaken to take firm grip upon the problem. Ratface was the man who'd driven that farm tractor out of the field. It was Plonker who rang him last night, Arnold had forgotten all about him. The rest of the lads had been out from London. Whether or not they wanted to, nobody here except Vennor knew how to get in touch.

Last night's meeting was brief. It took place quite late, in a quiet place, after Arnold, back from the hospital, had finally managed to telephone Plonker, and Ratface, when Plonker reminded him of the man's involvement, and Collie, just in from cruising around the town hoping to spot the two lads. Not a hope, of course.

They had agreed that nothing could be done there and then, and Arnold, wearing his unsought robe of command, ordered everybody home to bed. To bed, he said. No mucking about, no boozing. Meet again in the morning, when they'd had time to think. Bishop Adam Park.

So this morning they all went for a walk in the park, coming together where a clump of trees and unfruitful bramble bushes fringe the boating lake. Secretly, after a bad night all four would have liked to pull out; but no villain will let go of big tickle lightly, and none of them trusted the others not to spread the word if he did. At some time, the underworld would uncover most if not all of the truth about the job—those who had read the morning papers or listened to the local radio news would already be twitching noses and asking who did it—and what went for Arnold went for them all. A man dare not lose face, in their profession. So there they were, on this chilly, gray Sunday morning. Nobody else about, just a man walking his dog a long way off, on the other side of the lake.

This meeting, too, was brief. As Arnold said, they didn't want to be seen hanging about together, not with their form. And Vennor's orders were: Stay away from each other. Nobody else offering any worthwhile suggestion, he went on to say, "Listen—we've got to have another go at the hospital. We've got to see Mr. Vennor."

"Chancy," said Plonker Milgrave. They all agreed it was chancy; but as Arnold snapped, *anything* they did had to be chancy—including and especially sitting on their piles while the Old Bill ferreted. Delay they dared not.

"You'll have to do it, Collie," he said.

"Me?" said Collie. "Sod that. You're in charge."

"I went last night. People might notice, same face twice."

"Why not him?" Collie pointed at Ratface Rorke. "Or him." His thick finger moved on, pinpointing the Plonker.

"What's the bleeding difference?" Arnold snapped. "If he's awake and we have to go again, we'll take it in turns."

"Makes sense," said Plonker, and Ratface nodded. It got them out from under, for now at least, without loss of face.

Face. It kept Collie from more strenuous objection. He merely said, "What about if it's crawling with Old Bill?"

Valid point. They might have searched the wrecked car, empowered to or not. You never know what the sods are doing. "Do like you said yesterday," Arnold told him. "Peel off into a ward like you're visiting someone else. Keep close to a bunch of visitors."

"Better wait a little while, then," said Ratface. "Won't be many visitors early as this on a Sunday."

"Yeah. Yeah," Arnold agreed. "Better make it about twelve, half past." And he added, not without a certain satisfaction, "We'll all drive behind you, make sure you don't miss it."

The meeting was adjourned. It would reconvene at midday. Strict visiting hours have been abolished at St. Barnolph's. Quite a lot of people nip in before lunch on a Sunday, to get it out of the way before the telly really buckles to. Many patients, particularly the geriatric, request it. They prefer to spend the afternoon reliving the days of their sappy youth, sucking gums and liquorice allsorts over those old, old movies. And in the evenings, of course—though never on a Sunday— there's "Coronation Street," after they've listened to "The Archers." They lead a busy life, and they consume a lot of allsorts.

It is remarkable how soon a man who has every reason to be humming hymns of gratitude and relief after a narrow escape from death begins to gripe and cavil at the boredom surrounding recovery from it. Detective Inspector Rosher lay in his annex alive and tucked snugly away from a gray, chilly world, and he thought: Sod this. How long am I supposed to lie here, making shadow bunnies on the bloody wall?

Things were happening, outside. They'd brought the Sunday papers around, on a trolley. He'd bought one, and read in it the mention it gave to the robbery on the bypass. He wondered about this, flicking over mental photographs of local villains who could have been involved. Most likely, he thought, an out-of-town job, a city or Smoke mob who happened to choose that spot as suitable.

He wondered how Cruse was getting on with the black-boy case.

He wondered if the men who were sharing his work load between them had done all the things they ought to have done, leaving undone those things they ought not to have done.

He thought about Arnold Gutte. Funny, that.

He picked the paper up again, and looked for boxing news.

He gazed at the ceiling.

He thought: Sod it. How long, for Christ's sake, have I got to lie here?

His brown nurse was off duty, and he missed her. A friendless man in a lonely bed has need—mind you, this one would strenuously have denied it—for human contact, especially with a warm, feminine human; and she had warmth. So much of it that she had actually chipped the ice encasing his libido. He had felt . . . loneliness? Yes—a chill of disappointment, when he opened his eyes this morning and found breakfast being brought in by a Pakistani girl. He'd said at once, still fogged with sleep, "Where's Nurse Holness?"

"Off duty." Pleasant enough, this girl. But her personality lacked West Indian warmth. And she had nothing worth twitching for, in the way of buttock and bosom. "She'll be back this afternoon."

Sod it, he thought. And sod a bloody boiled egg. But better that than porridge.

8

On the way from Vennor's exceedingly desirable property to St. Barnolph's Cottage Hospital, Jack Hagger and his company passed a ruined church with a spire still standing, which must not be pulled down because it is a scheduled building. Nobody knows what it is scheduled for, but there it stands black and ruinous and dedicated to St. Thomas, who probably finds the bloody thing an embarrassment. Particularly the crypt, entered now through a jagged hole in the outer wall. Youthful graffiti are far from holy and the feet need to tread warily, because of shit and old condoms.

Winos sleep here sometimes, and the odd tramp uses it. Petty thieves hide bits of loot in it, but these people tend to avoid it nowadays, since a pack of herberts took it over. They meet there to sniff glue.

Some of the herberts were sniffing today, and one of them was big Billy Purvis—who emerged from the battered gate of the decrepit graveyard riding his high just as Hagger and henchman came driving along the street. Outside the gate Billy paused to dance a little, teetering on the edge of the curb.

"Watch dat geezer," said Georgie. Unnecessary warning to Hagger, who was driving. "All we need's to knock a pisser dahn."

He was right, of course. Unless you hit and run, knock a pisser down and you have to talk to policemen. Hitting and running was not on their agenda; it could prove a bothersome complication.

"I'm watching," Jack Hagger assured him. He was already steering wide, foot hovering near the brake in case the flapping, gyrating figure pranced into the roadway, to thumb his nose at the oncoming car or to fall with a whack off the curb.

Charles spoke. "Bit early, ain't it?"

"Sniff da bleetin' cork, dey're away, half of 'em," said Georgie. "Bleetin' turnip bashers."

Understandable, that they should believe the lad was drunk. The old generation relates it to drink, seeing this kind of behavior. High on glue is an adolescent variation. Works out cheaper—much cheaper than routine drugs—and is equally effective. They drove carefully by, leaving Billy dancing in the road behind them; dismissing entirely from their thoughts, having hardly admitted him, a lad who could have led them straight to what they were seeking, thus saving no end of bother. He didn't know himself, of course, what he had stashed last night in a heap of jalopies. But he knew where it was. It just goes to show.

When they reached the hospital they found, as they had expected, several cars in the visitors' park. Men in their line of business, where nasty accidents happen quite often, know about hospitals. The bell-tented lady had furnished them with the name of the room required. There would be direction boards inside. No need to all loom over the reception desk. Latch in behind a visiting party, close enough to be part of it. You have spoken to no one, in your London accent. You are part of the throng.

No problem at all. They mounted the stairs among three little parties: wife and mother-in-law of a perforated ulcer; husband and son of a urinary condition;

and the closer relatives of a retired delicatessen owner, said to be breathing his last. And so Inspector Rosher, gazing glumly through his door, saw three sharp-suited and snappy big men go by. Headed for the Ferguson Room. He said to himself, "Hello-ello-ello."

In under two minutes they came back, having penetrated the Ferguson Room, where a Chinese nurse engaged on room titivation (Matron is a tartar, every-thing has to *gleam*) told them Mr. Vennor was not here. He had been wheeled away with an oxygen bottle to Intensive Care. The one in the soft felt hat, rather slimmer and more gentlemanly than the others, raised it politely as he thanked her. They left; and when they passed this time, Inspector Rosher thought: They're bent. They're villains, I'll bet my pension on it.

A policeman knows. Thirty years of service under his belt? He knows. He knows.

I don't recognize them, he said to himself. They're from out of town. The city? Could be. Look of the Smoke about them.

Then came somebody he did know. Cauliflower Davis, passing by with his eyes fixed ahead. En route for that room. Or Sister's office. This was unlikely.

Cauliflower actually passed the Jack Hagger party on the stairs, but, busy with his nervous thoughts, he took no particular notice of them, any more than they, busy with their thoughts, did of him. He, too, had bypassed the reception desk—Arnold had briefed him—and he was poised for peeling off into a public ward should fuzz be around the corner at the head of the stairs.

No fuzz about that he could see. He hovered a mo-ment in the corridor, wondering if there was any inside the room. He could be walking straight into trouble.

The door stood slightly ajar. He listened intently at the crack, prepared to move away at a smart pace should anybody cough, or somebody speak in a masculine voice. From behind the door came a soft soprano humming, breaking into words now and again. Somebody singing, in an unknown tongue.

Singing? In a sickroom? A weird oriental ditty?

That wasn't right, it was out of kilter; and anything out of kilter is anathema to the sensitized bent engaged nefariously. Heart beating high, he turned away; turned back, stretching out a tentative hand to the doorknob; and all his veins jumped as it receded abruptly before his boggling eyes. The nurse came out, humming pianissimo.

She checked; not face to face with him because she was a tiny little thing, her slanted eyes level with the third button of his waistcoat. As startled as he was, she raised them, glossy black boot buttons, saying, "Ah. Can I help you?"

"Ah-ah," he replied. "No, I was just . . . Is Mr. Vennor in there?"

"He's been taken to the Intensive Care Unit."

"Intensive Care?"

"He deteriorated, I'm afraid. Are you with the other party?"

"Party?"

"The other men."

"Ah. Er . . . "

"They just left." Quite logically, because he exuded a similar ambience in his chalk-stripe suit (wear a suit, Arnold said; they all wear suits, hospital visitors), she assumed that he had become detached from the main party. People often do, they step aside into toilets.

"Ah," he said. "No, I'm—er—a friend."

"Well," she fluted in her high Hong Kong, "I'm afraid Mr. Vennor is not allowed visitors."

"Thank you, thank you." He turned; turned back. "How—er—how is he?"

"As comfortable as can be expected."

That's informative, if you like. "Ah," said Collie.

"Good. Yes. Thank you." He turned again. This time he hurried away.

Rosher was waiting for him. Unless he climbed out through a window, he had to come back. As the chalk-stripe suit came by his door, the inspector barked, "Collie!"

The Cauliflower stopped as if he had run into a wall. Old Blubbergut—it had to be Old Blubbergut! His fighter's head swiveled on his fighter's neck, his rubbery mouth dropped open. Jesus Christ! No mistaking that stern gorilla, with hard little eyes skewering him from under a bundle of bandage. Fucking Rosher, flat on his back with his leg in the air. "Ha ha ha," said Collie.

"Come in, lad, come in," the terrible shock barked. "Don't just stand there." And Collie found he had done it, he had moved forward into the sanitary room. The gorilla man spoke again.

"Visiting, are we?"

"Who, me?" said Collie. "No."

"What're you doing, then, half-inching drugs?" Half-inching: cockney rhyming slang for pinching. Almost obsolete. Hear a man use it, you can say he's over fifty.

"I mean—no—not here. I mean—got the wrong passage. Friend—in another ward."

"What ward?"

"Ah." Collie did not have one ready to the tongue. As most people do, guiltily disconcerted, he pulled bits out of the air. "Er—next floor. He's—er—he owes me a bit, I need it. Owes me a bit on a car deal. Flogged him a car, see." Subconscious connection, obviously. Vennor was in the car trade.

"Anybody I know?"

Again like most people hard pressed, Collie began to bluster. Villains automatically do it when faced with a probing policeman. They know their rights; but the bluster style tells a lot about the condition of their psyche at this moment. "You ain't got no right to ask me nothing, Mr. Rosher—"

"No," said Rosher. He wore now the expression of a great ape enjoying the sight of a bunch of fine bananas. "Just wondered. Any friend of yours is bound to be a friend of mine. Wouldn't be our little chum Arnold, would it? Didn't break a leg falling down the stairs last night, did he? On his way out of here."

"No—he—er—gotta be going." The big man turned, and was gone. Stuck fast in his bed, Inspector Rosher had no way of stopping him. No legal right to, either.

The three men from London had driven away by now. As they shut themselves into Jack Hagger's car, Georgie said, "Whadda we do now, den?"

"We have a drink." Hagger twisted the ignition key.

"Old Bill'll be all over the firken," said Charles.

As if Hagger had not already thought of that. All over the firken was, of course, an exaggeration. People wanting a policeman would experience the normal difficulty in finding one, people would get up, go for a walk in the park, watch football matches, fly kites, whistle at women, and never see one from start to finish. But certainly the pubs and watering places might expect a visit from men inquiring into the armed frolic on the bypass. Not all of them, mainly the ones where the bent foregathered; but in a strange town where you do not know which these are, better to avoid them all.

"We'll go into the country," he said.

Not long after, simply by following the road they were on, they arrived in the delightful small village of Hutton Fellows, which has a pub with thatch and a chestnut tree right on the main through route. "This'll do," said Hagger. "Maybe we can get a bite." It says "lunches" on a board outside, and they stick a menu in a little brass frame beside the rose-bordered door.

"Bit aht in de open, ayn't it?" Georgie, like all urban

criminals, misliked the open situation. Anonymity is sought by the townee in crowds. He feels conspicuous in isolation, it makes him uneasy.

Hagger, if he felt the stir of unease—possibly did, because he was a townee, too—hid it as a good leader must. The brain that won him that eminence had noted already the several cars parked outside, the general air proclaiming that here was a place geared for the tourist. And during the months when few tourists are about, strangers from the big city would drive out for pre-lunch Sunday drinks. "It'll do," he said. "They won't be looking for anything this far out."

The pub had stood there when worried men sat with leather tankards of ale arguing tactics best suited to lick the Armada. In those days it had little beamed bars, which survived war and pestilence and social upheaval right up to 1972. Good ale it served, too. But nothing survives a brewer's lust for profit. Now walls have been knocked down to make two big bars, and chemical fluids fizz out of electric pumps in an ambience of horse brasses, fake hunting prints, and plastic-wrapped pork pies. The beams have been painted in mat black to counterpoint vinyl-silk walls, and there is a jukebox. Also, a flashing, buzzing space-travel machine in the commoner bar which goes berserk when you hit Venus, depicted on the star-signs chart above as a naked lady with no arms to slap away hands that grope for her oversized bristols. These bristols flash when you hit her particular peg, poor lady.

The people from the parked cars stood about drinking a little of what they fancied, dressed in tweed and conversing loudly over the cacophonating jukebox in haw-haw voices. A few sat on little red-topped stools at the bar, shrieking appreciation of the saucy sallies lisped by the barman, called Jacques and queer as a bandicoot.

There were tables set about, with chairs around them. Hagger indicated one standing in the bow of the

Georgian window put in by the brewery because it prettified the outer façade and increased the customer capacity within at one fell swoop. While his minions crossed to be seated, the leader himself went to the bar. He said to Jacques, "Can we get lunch here?"

"Pies and sandwiches only, duckie," the barman told him. "Cook doesn't come on Sundays. Her husband's always complaining."

Shriek from the audience: a blond woman with black roots, too much makeup, and a poodle being fed cashew nuts out of one of the little glass dishes on the bar; three oddly assorted ladies, very tweedy, who might have been schoolteachers but then again might not; and two willowy young men who were probably lovers.

"Gin and tonic, lager and lime, pint of bitter, and half a dozen sandwiches," Hagger said.

"Ham or cheese?" the pretty pouf lisped, batting the pretty lashes. "I recommend the cheese, nothing like it to stiffen you up."

Another shriek. "Oo, Jacques," one of the tweedy ladies gurgled, "you *are* awful."

"It's your mind, duckie," said Jacques. "Never rises above the navel."

It crossed Hagger's mind that it would be nice to hammer the pouf's choppers down his pouffy throat. Nice; but very unwise, in this place at this time. So he said, quite mildly, "Three of each. I'll take the drinks with me."

He carried the glasses over to the table, where he shared them out: the pint of bitter to Georgie, the lager and lime to Charles, the gin to himself. He added tonic to his Gordon's and they all said cheers. Then they swigged or sipped according to potion, filling the time until the sandwiches arrived.

They came wrapped in plastic, decorated with a sprig of parsley on the side. Jacques put them down, saying, "There you are, dears. Tuck into those and you'll roar like a bull." He straightened up, held the tray in front of his delicate chest, and said to Charles, "My—aren't you *big*, duckie." His smile was coy, his lashes batted.

"Fuck orf," said the gentleman's gentleman.

"Charming," the barman said. He flounced away, pouting. The three men unwrapped three sandwiches and clogged up their teeth with steam-baked bread.

"So," said Georgie, through cheese. It had to be cheese, you could see the pasty-colored sliver between the slices. Ham is pink. "What you gonna do?"

"He's got a business, hasn't he?" Hagger said. He ate more delicately, but not so delicately as Charles, who sipped at his lager and lime with a little finger stuck out. "Garage business. We'd better have a look at it."

"Where is it?" Georgie asked. He really was a messy eater.

"Can't remember the address, offhand." But he has a garage, I had him checked. "Charles—there's a phone box on the green. Fifty yards along the road."

"I'll have to have your ball-point," Charles said. "And I'll tear a bit orf the phone book. Look after me lager."

He got up and left the pub. The jukebox howled, the standing people haw-hawed. Over at the bar the little audience was shrieking gladly. Jacques, recovering quickly as a good pro will, was at it again. All very merry. Hagger and Georgie chomped on doggedly, leaving their colleague's share wrapped in the shiny plastic. Charles came back. He said, "There's three businesses under Vennor. I put 'em all dahn."

Hagger took the proffered piece of paper torn from the directory. The careful capitals spelled out: Vennor, E: Import and Export; Vennor, E: Automotive Spares; and Vennor Garages. There was only one, but the man intended to open more. Addresses were appended. The three businesses were in different parts of the town. He said, "Good. We'll take a look at the garage first. Scoff your sandwich, Charles, while I square up with the pouf."

Two policemen came in a panda car along the road that forms a T-junction with the street fronting St. Thomas's ruinous church. They were on routine patrol, cruising a patch where nothing much happens on a Sunday. On the corner where the two roads meet a big youth danced, arms flapping as he gyrated, singing at the top of his voice. When the car drew in to the curb and one of the policemen got out, the dancer stuck up two fingers at him.

"All right," the policeman said when he was close enough, "that'll be enough of that."

"Bollicks," the youth said, and carried on with his dancing.

"I think you'd better come along with me," said the policeman.

"Hah! Hah! Hah!" replied the youth, and began to feint and weave, making karate chops. The policeman delivered one short but quite sweet right hook. Rosher would have appreciated it. The youth lay down on the pavement.

The other policeman came out from the car. "Give us a hand with him, Wally," said the one with the sweet right hook. "We'll run him down to the station."

Arnold Gutte, having driven behind Cauliflower Davis's car to the hospital, waited for him in Bishop Adam Park. Later he would ring Plonker Milgrave and Ratface Rorke, to pass on whatever needed to be passed and to fix time and place for a further meeting. But only if strictly necessary, on this they all agreed, as they had all agreed that Arnold alone should see Collie to the hospital. Villains touched with panic see policemen behind every tree. They might have found out about last night's gathering, being crafty bastards. Mr. Vennor had said: Keep separate. Without doubt, he made sense. Every meeting added to the dangers.

So Arnold sat alone in his car on the edge of the park, and when Collie drove along he got out and walked along a path leading all the way down to the boating lake, through the scrubby woods. Collie joined him there, undeniably under severe strain. He blurted at once, "Fucking Rosher's in there."

"In where?" said Arnold, looking all around. They were in a clearing; and who could tell what crouched among the undergrowth?

"In the hospital."

"Rosher is? The copper Rosher?"

"Right next to Mr. Vennor's room."

"Oo fuck. Guarding it?"

"No—he's in bed. Got his leg up."

"Got his leg up? Up where?"

"He seen me. He seen you."

"I wasn't there."

"Last night. When you went in."

"Oo fuck," said Arnold.

"He's sniffing. He's asking questions."

"Did you talk to him, then?"

"Couldn't help it, could I? He seen me before I seen him. Didn't have no option."

"What did he say?"

"Nothing much. Asked if I was visiting. I said a friend. In one of the wards. Said he'd seen you."

"That all?"

"I got out of it, didn't I?"

"Didn't he stop you?"

"I keep telling you, don't I? He's got his leg up. All bandages round his head."

"Patient, is he?"

"Course he fucking is. In bed, ain't he, in this room. Next to Mr. Vennor. And *he's* in Intensive Care. And some other geezers been in to see him, she thought I was part of 'em. Just left, they had—"

"Hang about, hang about," said Arnold. "Let's get it all in order."

He made Collie tell him just what had happened. When the story was done, he said, "Fucking hooray," and thought awhile. At length he said, "He can't get up, then, Rosher?"

"Got his leg all plastered."

"What happened to him?"

"I don't know, do I?"

Neither of them had had time to read last evening's local paper, which carried an account of the plane crash—spread it big, death of local solicitor and well-known police inspector injured—but they'd been very busy. Arnold spoke again. "We'd better not stand about here. Let's move on."

They followed the path on toward the lake. Collie said, "I reckon we ought to turn it up. Get clear."

This is exactly what Arnold wanted to do, with all his wicked heart and soul. Two factors now held him. First, this matter of face. Give a man a measure of sudden power, and whatever stresses come with it he swells at the ego. This was his first taste of leadership, and he found he liked it. He was getting ideas about his future. Pull this off and, well, people would know, he would be respected, admired. He could run his own gang. Nothing too big, to start with; but later... Chicken now, crack now, and there was no future. No face left.

The other factor: it takes money, to go underground. People have to be paid, or they turn you in. And they don't come cheap. He didn't have that kind of money.

Also: what about the wife, the mortgage, all the domestic bit? He could trust her—so long as he kept a reasonable quota of cash and goodies flowing in. But ditched suddenly—he couldn't take her with him, even if she'd go; which he doubted—and left with it all on her back, no money supply—what would she do? Shop him, was his guess. Not for this job designed to set them both on gravy, she didn't know a thing about it (although she might start to wonder, if he vanished and they found that jalopy) but there were bits and pieces in his house that the Old Bill would be happy to cast a beady eye upon; and some of them would point to other people.

That would be fatal. That could send him to the knacker's yard.

He said, "How bad did Rosher look?"

"Bloody horrible," said Collie. "Always does, don't he? Like a bleeding great monkey."

"I don't mean that. I mean, he's not likely to be out any minute, is he?"

"How the fuck do I know? He *looked* set."

"Listen," said Arnold. "I've been thinking. It's my bet Mr. Vennor had them lads take that jalopy to his garage. Meant to move it on, or something. But he couldn't, could he? So it'll still be there. Won't it?"

"So'll the pigs, if Rosher's tumbled. He'll get on the blower, won't he? They bring it to your bedside."

"Why should he have tumbled?" But he might. He was cunning. Oh, cunning and hard. They were *all* cunning. "Listen—they wouldn't have had time to sort it all out yet, would they? You only left a quarter of an hour ago. All right—we go and take a look at the garage."

"Sod that," said Collie.

"A *look*. We don't even have to go in. We just go and take a look."

"I don't—"

Arnold looked his follower straight in the eye. Had to tilt his head back a little to do it. "You chicken?" he demanded. Just like that.

Collie bridled at once. Face is a burden at all levels. "You wanna fucking watch it," he said.

"Come on, then. We'll go in your car." Arnold led the way back along the path. If anybody was taking license plate numbers, he'd sooner it wasn't his. Perhaps something of the leader was in him, at that.

9

The two policemen, P.C. Wally War-
grave and P.C. Gordon Kenton, realized even as they
bent over to pick him up that Billy Purvis was not
drunk. The fumes emanating from a drunk can lift the
cap off a constable at close range. The caps of these two
men stayed firmly in place. Wally Wargrave said,
"He's been sniffing. Glue all down his shirt, look, the
dirty little bugger."

"He'll have been at the church," said Gordon
Kenton. "Want to have a look up there? See who else is
about?"

"No, leave 'em." Glue sniffing was not an offense, in
the eyes of the law. "Let's load this one and take him
in."

They lugged the supine Billy over to the car as young
Mike Gibbins came from a side street a little further up
on the opposite side of the road. Billy should have
called for him an hour ago, they had to deliver the car
he was driving to thick punter, and then they were due
to try out a newly souped machine at a stock car meet.
Surely the twat's not sniffing? he'd thought. Not at a
time like this. And knowing where to look he came to
find out, fuming. Seeing the situation, he went past
with his hair prickling all over and turned to vanish
along another tributary street. The steering on that

car was not all the punter would think it until he'd driven it five hundred miles, but it turned corners.

Billy came around as he was inserted into the back of the patrol car, and began immediately to sing again. "I'll get in with him," said Wally Wargrave, "in case he goes bonkers." Standard practice. A drunk, a junkie, a sniffer, or a plain old-fashioned nutter amuck in the back with two coppers trapped in the front seats can give rise to grave mayhem, and pursed lips among the upper brass.

The big lad gave no trouble. The urge to dance seemed to have left him, and he was content to sing and giggle all the way to the police station. Even when they off-loaded and steered him into the little reception area he came without protest.

A leather-covered bench runs along one wall of the reception hall. They walked him over and sat him down upon it. He lolled back, giggling. P.C. Kenton stayed, to catch him if he did as he might have done, and toppled off onto his head. The bruised subject tends nowadays to charge the police with brutality. P.C. Wargrave crossed to the small glassed-in box of an office within which Sergeant Barney Dancey spent contented shifts. He was there now.

"Got a little one for you, Barney," Wally Wargrave said.

Barney. Everybody called him Barney; except the schoolchildren who looked right, left, and right again before crossing the road, urged to it in his road safety lectures. They called him Uncle Barney and wished they had him at home instead of their fathers. Even the silly little sods who looked right, left, and right again before stepping straight under a passing car attached no personal blame to him. He cast his mild blue eye over Billy now, and then he looked at Wally Wargrave. "Glue?" he said.

"The original Bostick boy. Obstruction, obscene language, attempting to strike an officer. Karate chopper, he is. Disturbing the peace, he sings like a bloody warthog."

Barney sighed, very regretfully. "They will do it. Put him in the cells, let him cool off a bit?"

"Come on, Barney—I want him in the book. I've got nothing in it this week, all my regulars must have died." A man needs a few arrests in his book. How else can he prove he was working? A quiet patch, in all common sense, should be seen as tribute to the policing of it. And yet a policeman normally feels a sort of guilt, if his book goes in day after day unsullied.

"Up to you, lad," said Barney, and he reached for his big black incidents tome. "Fetch him over."

Constable Kenton urged tittering Billy to his feet. He sheep-dogged him over. "Don't touch him, Barney," he warned. "We might have to steam you off."

Barney addressed the lad regretfully. "All right, lad. Let's have your name and address."

"Bollicks," said Billy, and he giggled like a fool.

"See what I mean?" said Wally Wargrave. "He's done it again."

"Take him down to Ernie," Barney said. "We'll get his details when he comes down a bit. Better have his personal effects. Don't worry, son, we're just going through your pockets, see you can't damage yourself." Ernie was P.C. Ernest Gilmore, in charge of the dungeons below.

And all this time, Inspector Rosher was lying in his bed, thinking.

Arnold Gutte and Cauliflower Davis arrived at their fallen chieftain's garage while Gentleman Jack Hagger and his henchmen were finishing lunch, out at Hutton Fellows, the population of which, incidentally, dwindled by one when Mr. Henry Croker, a distinguished inhabitant, having attempted a robbery similar in some respects to their own, went to jail for it.

Collie driving, they came along the street, stopping at some distance and sitting there for some little time, to survey the situation.

"Quiet enough," Arnold said at length. "Let's drive on—go into the forecourt."

"I don't like it," said Collie. "I really don't. They're crafty bastards. How do we know they ain't staked out? They might be watching us already."

Arnold, the leaning toward leadership taken good hold by now, felt for his colleague with the cauliflower ear the affectionate contempt proper in generals toward the lower orders. What is more, as this sense of his own superiority increased he felt self-doubt dwindling. This mental phenomenon is the factor that brings to calamity more mob leaders than the police, unaided by it, ever could; just as it killed more men on the Somme and at Mons and other French places than could have been managed by their own efforts. He said, "They're not here, I'll bet you on it. We'll go up to the pumps, as if we want to fill up."

"There's nobody on the fucking pumps."

"I know that, don't I?" The pensioner did not work on Sunday. "So we get out, fiddle with the nozzles, and nip into the yard if there's no sign of life."

"I don't like it. You said we didn't have to go in."

"Come on, for Christ's sake."

They drove into the forecourt and stopped by the pumps. Nobody about. Eyes flickering around, they fiddled for a moment or two. Then Arnold said, "Come on," and slipped through the gate into the yard. Collie followed.

The yard wore its Sunday air of morose and brooding squalor. The great heap of scagged and dented stripped carcasses over by the canal fence gloomily awaited tomorrow, when the crane, silent now, would pick them up one by one in its magnetized iron jaws and swing a dinosaurus neck to the crusher, which would squash them down into tidy square packages. The ground between here and there was littered with old oil drums, clapped axles, gearboxes, a moribund engine or two—all the greasy clutter of your average scrapyard. A gray waste under a gray sky, not lightened even by the varicolored cellulosed heap.

"What are we supposed to be doing, then?" Collie asked. He was whispering, although, for sure, nobody was about.

"Looking for the jalopy, ain't we?" Arnold, too, kept his voice low, and very small.

"It ain't here, is it? It won't be here." All Collie desired was to get out of this. He was turning to the gate already.

"Haven't bleeding looked, have we?" Arnold hissed it savagely. Nothing like savage hissing to fetch a qualmish minion into line. "Where would you put it, if you wanted to hide a banger?"

"That sod Rosher'll have rung 'em, won't he?" said Collie. "He'll have give 'em a bell, they'll be here any minute."

But Arnold was pointing, saying, "Over there. Strip it down, shove it with all them jalopies. Come on."

"They'll be on their way, won't they?"

"Better bleeding hurry, then, hadn't we? Come on." Arnold was moving already, across the oily wasteland. The Cauliflower followed, but not with alacrity.

When they reached the great, pathetic stack— somebody had loved every one of those cars, once. Had polished them religiously, taken the family out for runs, proposed in them, fornicated in them, drunk coffee out of flasks in lay-bys, cursed the lack of toilets on main roads as they rushed along praying they might find one in time; choked in the throat, perhaps, when the poor old beastie was hauled away at last to this knackery—Arnold said, "What color was it? The jalopy."

"I don't know. Never see it, did I?" True enough. The car in which Collie had traveled to the barn had paused outside only long enough to collect the renegade guard and the guns. Nobody from it had really entered the barn, where the jalopy stood.

Arnold cast his mind back. "Blue. It was blue. Look for a blue Hillman."

"They're *all* bloody blue," Collie said.

They were not, of course. He was seeing them through the eyes of a man needing badly to be gone. There were reds and yellows and psychedelics, and one in purple and green. But this is true: a lot of blue ones rusted among them. Light blues, medium blues, two-tone blues, dark blues; and some with the piebald patina that comes only after many years of standing outside in all the British weathers. Arnold said, "Dark blue. Look at all the dark blue ones."

"I won't bleeding know it if I see it," said Collie, no longer whispering. Even he could tell that nobody was here.

Perhaps Vennor's idea was not so brilliant after all. Arnold had no enormous brain, but it had not taken him long to tumble. Be fair, though—the jalopy should have been relieved of its baubles by now, all stripped down and ready for mashing.

"You start here, I'll start there," said Arnold. "All you got to do is tell me if you see a dark blue Hillman."

"What are we supposed to do," Collie demanded, "lift 'em up with our bare hands? You can only see the ones on top."

"Get on with it, for Christ's sake. It'll *be* on top, won't it?" Arnold walked to the other side of the stack and began to peer.

The blue banger, of course, was not among the top layer. There were a few Hillmans, since even this marque, noted for longevity, limps to the grave at last. Arnold knew at once that the one sought was not among those he spotted; but every time Collie observed one it meant a walk all the way around the stack, to dismiss it—the stupid fellow was calling attention to obvious outsiders—and all the way back again. This takes time.

And time was of the essence, with policemen possibly en route and Jack Hagger and his men on the way. Although, of course, the Vennor boys didn't know this.

At just about the time when Hagger was asking a man who just happened to be walking about in a suburb how one gets to Scone Road, where Vennor's garage was situated, Detective Inspector Alfred Stanley Rosher began to unwind the turban of bandages swathing his durable skull. He had just put down the telephone, brought to his bed when he asked for it after a time of solid thinking.

Had his Sunday newspaper made more fuss of the bypass robbery story he might have connected it immediately with the passing of his door, last night by Arnold Gutte and this morning by three sharp-suited men certainly bent, followed by Arnold's friend Cauliflower Davis: all headed for the Ferguson Room. And then from it. As it was, when Collie left in a hurry he lay back, thinking. Something funny was going on.

What?

He knew why the visits had been so brief. That much was obvious. They came to see Vennor; but Vennor wasn't there, he had been moved to the Intensive Care Unit.

So: they were not close enough to have known. They had not been notified that Vennor was too ill to see visitors. The three men, therefore, were not likely to be relatives. Arnold Gutte and Cauliflower Davis certainly were not.

A friend, Collie had said. He'd come to see a friend, owed him money on a car deal.

Discount that. Shocked, he blurted the first thing that came into his thick head.

But: in a shocked blurting is very often an element of truth. A car deal.

Wasn't this bloke Vennor in the car business?

Any car deal involving Collie—and Arnold Gutte? He'd come, too—was more than likely bent.

So: was Vennor bent?

Very profitable, the car caper. And he, presumably, had all the usual connections throughout the trade— in the car caper there are bent cartels—plus facilities to respray, change number plates, get hold of logbooks, generally tart and titivate. That and a few boys working with bits of malleable wire is all you need. It's the easiest lurk on earth.

Had he, then, Detective Inspector Alfred Stanley, been given hint of a car caper, even as he lay here in this bum-numbing bed?

The three out-of-towners. Did they fit in?

Mmm. If they were street operators, or members of a cartel owed money: too soon after Vennor's accident to come panicking after him. They couldn't collect anyway. Could they? Not here. He wouldn't have his mattress stuffed with poppy, and the bent shun checks.

Even if they were wielders of the malleable wire and had cars for him: why come here? Why risk it? They'd switch to another outlet. Plenty of them, plenty of crook dealers.

Hmm.

Then a small spark fizzed. What about that caper on the bypass?

No. Too big for Arnold and the Cauliflower.

But the sharp boys? London?

No. Nothing was missing from the van, the paper said. Whoever was engaged wouldn't hang around here.

Mm. They had that indefinable something that plants London in the mind.

Perhaps they were *collecting* from Vennor. Upper-bracket vehicles. Heard about the accident, came to try—something. A word to tell them where the cars were. Something.

He pressed his little bell, and the Pakistani nurse came. He said, "Three big men, smart suits. Went along toward the Ferguson Room this morning. Did you see 'em?"

"No," she said. "Can't say I did." She had a brother called Muhammad Ali, but he was five feet tall.

"Who was on duty there, do you know?"

"Nurse York, I think. She was tidying up the room after Mr. Vennor went."

"Is she about? I'd like a word with her."

"I'll see. I think she's on lunches, she'll be washing up." Oh yes—if the poor little things can't con a walking patient into it, at St. Barnolph's hospital they do the washing up.

Are the Chinese truly a very happy race, or is it simply their misfortune that they look that way? Nurse York came cheerfully in. She said, beaming merrily, "Hallo. Did you want to see me?"

"Yes. You were on duty in the Ferguson Room. Three big men came."

"That's right."

"What did they want?"

"Well—to see the patient. But he wasn't there, he'd gone."

"Did they say why? I mean—who they were, or anything?"

"No. Another man came after, said he was a friend."

"What did they sound like? The first three."

"London," she said promptly. "They're London. I know, I lived in London. Gerrard Street, do you know it?"

"Uh-hn," he said. "Thank you. Can I have a telephone?" Unless he watches it and works at it constantly, in a hospital the most piggish of chauvinists reduces to suppliant. They have ways to soften him up, these tender-boiled nurses. Like simply not doing whatever he barks to have done. A sweating hour left without the bottle will reduce any man to cringing. So Rosher added, "Please."

"You're a detective, aren't you?" she said, angled eyes beaming worldwide goodwill. She didn't look like the Yellow Peril. "Are they bad men?"

"Telephone," he said; and because the beaming ones are often the toughest, and he really did want to make that call, he added again, "Please."

She went away, and must have passed his request on. Possibly to have obliged him herself would have been unethical. Every profession has its code. The telephone came with the Pakistani girl, complete with extension lead. She plugged it in, gave it to him, and hovered.

"Do you mind?" he said. "It's private business." She went, to wonder with the Chinese girl what policemanly thing he was up to. He extended a thick finger, and dialed.

"Central Police Station," the instrument said.

"Barney?" He'd recognized the voice.

"Is that you, Alf?" More instant recognition. No magic about it. The phone often was switched through to Barney Dancey's reception desk, on a Sunday; and Inspector Rosher, once heard, was seldom forgotten. Barney, that good man, had listened to him over many years and was the only person in the world who called him Alf. His fat wife had; but if she mentioned him at all nowadays in the house where she lived with her even fatter mother, she called him Him, and in her mind: the bastard. Nor was she alone in this.

"Yes."

"How are you? I'll be in to see you as soon as I get the chance."

He would, too. He'd be in, though nobody else came nigh. "Fine, fine," said Rosher. "Is Young Alec about?"

"No. He's working today, but he's off on his tod. Following up the black-boy business."

"Any progress there?" This as a by-the-way. Because of the lad's sister, because of his ingrained professionalism, he had interest in the matter; but his main thinking wove around the other peculiar business.

"If there is I haven't heard about it. They tell me the lad's sister is your nurse."

"Uh-huh."

"Percy's in his office, if you want a word with him."

"No. It doesn't matter. You might ask Young Alec to give me a tinkle, when he comes in." Detective Inspector Young Alec Cruse he would speak to, outlining the situation; but Chief Superintendent (Percy) Fillimore: no. Never. Percy had been known, often, to absorb the work of another officer junior in rank, act upon it, and claim the successful outcome as his own unaided work. As bitter enemy of long standing, he'd never had the chance to do it to Rosher. He was not getting it now, free to grab all the kudos, if such there were, while Alfred Stanley lay immobilized and raging in a hospital bed. Not bloody likely, and sod what the book might say.

"Who's got this job on the bypass?" he asked.

"Percy."

"Busy little bugger, isn't he?" More reason than ever to button the lip. In times of stressful overwork, Percy looked thinly down his nose at vague suspicion presented by men—oh, and especially Rosher—who would add to his load. Hard proof is what he demanded. So sod him.

"Time of the year," said Barney. Probably joking, because there is no close season in crookery. He said it, anyway. "Not much in the bypass caper, I reckon. They left all the stuff in the truck."

"Mm," said Rosher. "Don't say I was asking, but what do you know about a bloke called Vennor?"

"He's in with you, somewhere." This sort of question the man in charge of the Incidents Book can answer off the cuff. "Came unstuck on the main road, hit a lorry.

Hang on, I've got the bumf here somewhere." A short silence. "Mm . . . here we are—Vennor, Elton. Nature of incident—"

"Aye, but what does he do?"

"Ah. Well—he's Chamber of Commerce chairman, isn't he? Got a couple of businesses—two or three—can't remember offhand—"

"One a garage?"

"Yes. Vennor Garages. Big place, Scone Road. Got a spares business, too."

"Anything on the file?"

"No. Well, I can check. But—no."

"Mm." There was no apparent reason why Rosher should ask his next question. Policemen with stiffening antennae seem sometimes to gather vibrations out of the ether. "What was he driving?"

"Vauxhall, it says here. P registration. OYX 272 P."

"Uh-huh."

"What's up?"

"Nothing. Nothing. Just—you know—need something to think about, lying here. Ta, Barney. See you."

"I'll be in," said Sergeant Barney. "Might even bring some grapes." What's the old sod up to? he wondered as he put the phone down.

Inspector Rosher was, in fact, lying back with the telephone on his stomach and a concentrated scowl on his corrugated-leather simian face. Chairman, Chamber of Commerce. P-registered Vauxhall. That wasn't right. Was it? An ambitious and well-to-do businessman with open sesame to garage and dealer trade discounts has the pick of the market. By perks, by inclination, for image-building he drives something expensive and glittering. A Porsche, a Mercedes, a Rolls. With personalized number plates, most likely.

He doesn't bang about in an aging mass-produced Vauxhall.

Unless, of course, he'd just bought it in and was testing. Or his own machine was out of action. Because the very best go off the road at times, sticking water pump or something.

But: he'd have the pick of his stock, as temporary replacement. And the pick, surely, wouldn't be a P-registered Vauxhall?

Forget the bypass caper. It had gone wrong anyway. If London herberts were involved, they wouldn't still be here, visiting hospitals.

Cars. Lots of money in it.

Why did he ask what car the man was driving? He didn't really know. But this he did know: if his nose made him ask it, his nose had its reasons.

This is when he said, violently: sod it, and curving himself up in the bed he laid hold of the thick white leg, which stabbed him with pain as he eased it out of the sling. He maneuvered until he was sitting on the edge of the mattress; and then he began to unwind the turban.

He was out of the hospital pajamas, into his underpants, and shoving one arm into his shirt when the nurse came back to remove the telephone. He shot a darkling glance sideways at her, as if warning that, crossed, he would beat the matted hair on his barrel chest and jump up and down, gibbering. Never had she seen such a hairy man. Or such a bulging crotch. She cried, "Mr. Rosher—what are you doing? Where do you think you're going?"

"Home," he barked.

"You can't do that," she said. "You can't do that." And receiving no answer, as he bent to retrieve trousers from the bedside locker, she shot out of the room.

By the time she returned with Sister he was doing up the old-fashioned button fly of those durable blue serge trousers, lower half of a durable blue serge suit. The passing of the button fly is a matter for regret, especially among unfortunates struggling to free zip from pubic hair in the name of progress. Sister, a lady who needed neither steel nor whalebone in her corset, said like a whetted knife, "Mr. Rosher, get back in that bed at once!"

He did not say bollicks, except in his mind. He said, "Make me."

"We can't have this," she said. "How can we run a hospital?"

He eased the braces over his heavyweight's shoulders—what a pity his legs were so short and bandy; and furry with it—making no reply. He reached for his tie, one foot in sock, the other clumped in plaster. Very painful. She snapped, "Nurse—fetch Dr. Harker."

The nurse scurried away. Sister stood drawn up stiffly in a hissing silence. He finished his knotting and picked up his jacket, neatly folded in the little deal cupboard. The nurse scurried back. "Dr. Harker is off," she said. "He's gone on a Methodist outing."

"In that case," Sister said, "fetch Dr. Bancroft." The nurse shot away again.

A new silence, while he donned his jacket and looked for his shoes. They stood tidily, side by side, beneath the cupboard. "I'm discharging myself, Sister," he said, thinking: I'll have to wear one, carry the other.

"We'll see about that," she said.

Dr. Bancroft must have been near at hand because the nurse whizzed back with him now. He showed no sign of breathlessness, no sweat shone on him, so he could not have come far. He arrived, in fact, quite unhurriedly and addressed Sister, ignoring the patient as completely as if he had been an old-age pensioner here under the National Health.

"What's wrong, Sister?"

"This patient, Doctor. Mr. Rosher. He says he is discharging himself."

The doctor—pleasant-looking man he was, quite young—glanced at Rosher, smiled a little, and said, "Well—let him."

"He has head injuries." Sister was bridling, as at a personal affront.

"It's his head. What's today? Sunday, is it?" He sent his smile toward Rosher. "Come in tomorrow, we'll take a squint. He'll need crutches, Sister, by the look of it."

"I'm not sure that we have any suitable—"

"In that case, he'll have to hop." And the doctor vanished. Rosher, who had never seen him before, never saw him again.

They fitted him out with crutches. There was a goodly selection, Sister had spoken out of umbrage. Buttoning his battleship-gray raincoat, he said, "I suppose you can ring for a cab?"

Sister was still around. She snapped, "I hardly think your superiors will be pleased by—"

He was doing the thing that people who knew him dreaded. He was producing a great handkerchief which, her kill-germ mind noted as it appeared, needed a damn good boiling. "I'll worry about that, madam," he snapped in reply. "You stick with the Ex-lax." And he blew.

She stiffened, with her eyes popped. As did the Pakistani nurse's. A porter bringing an aged lady back to the ward next door after examination ran her wheelchair into the wall. She sat there cursing cruelly, even her stone-deafness penetrated, and a bird about to alight on the windowsill fell backward and had to flap like crazy before it could zoom away with hammering heart, inches only above the ground.

It takes a little time, to resettle after a shock like this. All unaware, Inspector Rosher mopped up, coughed, replaced the handkerchief, and found he had to bend his head sideways (because the crutch was under his arm) to scratch the tenpenny-piece-sized pink tonsure that sat right on the crown of his cannonball head, marring the perfection of a classic short-back-and-sides haircut. When he was finished, Sister addressed the Pakistani girl.

"Ring for a cab, Nurse. Tchah."

She turned on her sensible heel and swept out with a rustle. Not one word of farewell. Trades union officials, post office counter clerks, traffic wardens, and hospital sisters can forgive much. But never a gratuitous offense against the dignity of their powerful calling.

Five minutes later the Pakistani nurse conducted Inspector Rosher to the lift. She stayed with him as he inexpertly crutched his pottery across the reception hall, down the steps, and into the cab, from the backseat of which he gruffed, "Thank you, Nurse. Don't do anything I wouldn't." Not blessed with social grace, he found difficulty always when he had to utter thanks or make farewell. Hence the cliché. It expressed goodwill.

"Good-bye, Mr. Rosher," she said. "Don't forget to come tomorrow, for your checkup. Call at the office, they'll give you a card."

Bugger the office. He gave the address of his house on the hill and the driver let the clutch in. The inspector sat back, wondering what means to adopt for shifting from his pocket to the public purse the cost of this taxi.

Well, he was out; but sod it—how was he going to follow anything up? He couldn't drive, and hobbling on crutches, he had already found, was painful. His shoulder muscles ached after just a few yards, his ribs hurt, his leg stabbed pain. Maybe he should have stayed where he was, passed his thought on to Percy, as per the book.

But sod Percy. He might pooh-pooh it all. He'd done it before. And if he didn't, how bloody maddening to provide the means by which he accrued kudos.

Chancy, though, to throw away the book. He'd had enough trouble.

He thought upon these things as the cab ran down

toward the town center; and suddenly a gleam came into his hard little eye and the corners of his grim mouth turned upward. Gave the driver a nasty turn, when he glanced in the rearview mirror.

He'd had a bang on the head. It still ached a bit. A person with a bang on the head may be expected to have lapses, to indulge in unconventional activity. Only to be expected. Such persons had been known even to discharge themselves from the hospital.

He leaned forward as best he could with his heavy leg stuck out before him, and spoke to the driver.

"Cancel that address. Go to Sharman Street. I'll pick out the house when we get there."

If the taxpayer was buying the ride, he'd just make a little call on Arnold Gutte.

10

Arnold and his associate Cauliflower Davis were still among the jalopies when Jack Hagger arrived with his merry men, one of them sucking a mint to combat wind caused by Mother's Relish steam-baked bread consumed with the plastic cheese. Bolder than the local men, and as big-time Londoners contemptuous of small-town police, they drove straight into the forecourt, seconds only after Georgie said: Dere it is, look, and pointed to the name above the garage. Which the others had already seen.

They got out of Hagger's smart borrowed saloon (the police in London were just taking its particulars from a very upset owner), and Charles shifted the mint from his tongue to say, "Somebody here already?" Because standing by the pumps was Collie's car. "Wouldn't be the pigs, would it?"

He spoke without undue concern. It certainly was not a police car. The pigs have been known to drive their own private vehicles, using them as camouflage; but they were not here. And if they came—so what? Jack Hagger showed equal unconcern as he said, "So who cares? No law against looking for spares."

"What we going to do, then," Charles asked, "now we're here?"

Had he been less of a leader, Hagger would have

admitted that he was not quite sure. He'd come to this yard mainly because the sudden knocking awry of all those well-knit plans, the abrupt confusion surrounding the entire project, the threatened snatching from under his nose of more loot than most of the bent ever see in one place throughout their entire career, hammered at the two mainsprings of his character: greed and pride.

He simply could not accept that Vennor's accident had killed the matter off—not with all that tickle still around somewhere. No way could he bring his men all this way out from London, only to trundle them meekly home again. That's a great way to destroy a hard-won image of infallibility.

More implacably even than it threatened Arnold, the jungle law that prevails in the underworld glared him in the eye. He must not lose face. At the heels of every criminal leader the young ambitious upstart drools, ready at the first sign of frailty to tear him down; as often as not enlisting the leader's own henchmen to set him up. On his own level are his fellow predators, greedy and ruthless as himself and more than willing to eliminate him for the sake of his lucrative business.

And apart from face, he had money and time invested in the job. He had paid that guard already, and back in London the lads who did the raiding awaited their cut. It had to be paid. And he could afford to pay it. But it went savagely against the grain, to pay and not collect. That was failure, on every level.

And the bloody gear was around here, somewhere. Around this town. In a car. That much he knew, and that only. Vennor had outlined the method, and it was good. Obvious, really, given his facilities. The loot in a car, the car away, the loot off-loaded, the car driven innocently away to the crusher. Gone, before the pigs had time to act upon any eye-witness descriptions.

But what car? Was it the one he'd been driving? Or

another, stashed temporarily until he moved it here; which he never had, having piled up too soon.

No. Discount the car in which he clouted the truck. The man was too canny to drive the stuff around in person. And a second car had been abandoned in the city, so it wasn't in that. And the third car was his, and it came home.

So what car? And where was it?

Here? Possibly. The plan would have been, surely, for it to be brought here? But Vennor had not filled in all the details, it had not seemed important. Hagger's direct involvement was with the actual raid. And his cut. Which he had not got. Now he said, in answer to Charles, "Look at motor cars. What we want is one with a false bottom to the tank."

"How do we tell, den?" Georgie asked.

"Use your knuckles. It ought to sound more hollow." Would it? He didn't really know. He nodded to the gate giving entry to the yard. "If it's about, it will be in there."

"Whadda we do if de pigs come?" This from Georgie.

"We'll handle that when it happens."

His own bet said that it wouldn't. Not so closely involved as Arnold, and with a far better leader's brain, he saw the matter more objectively. If the police believed, as they were intended to, that the raiders had panicked and left the truck's cargo where it stood, they would not be too interested. Panicking villains get well clear, the local police would believe that nothing was left on their territory. No reason why they should connect Vennor's boomps-adaisy with the raid, miles away. And they could not know about the stash car. So why should they come here? But—just in case—he said to Georgie as they approached the gate, "Take a squint through the crack, before you open it."

Now, this is leadership. Though you can perform a minor task as easily yourself, command that a minion do it. It emphasizes your eminence, many a mickle making a muckle; and it provides constant check. If he does it at once, no hesitation: you are firm in the saddle. If he demurs: check your armaments.

Georgie did not demur. He applied an eye and roved it around, across the very spot where, seconds before, Arnold had been bent over, peering to see what he could of car carcasses under the top layer. But Arnold had just been called to the other side of the stack, where Collie thought he saw another Hillman. "Looks all clear to me," said Georgie.

They opened the gate and came through. Ahead was the littered, oil-scummy ground, the heap of carcasses and the fence. Beyond, on the other side of the canal, nothing but the blind eyes of a crumbling warehouse long abandoned and a bristle of television aerials, obviously attached to roofs that hid below the fence line. To their left, on concrete in front of the workshop building, stood two cars left for tinkering. They turned left. Behind the carcasses, Collie was saying, "Fuck this. It ain't here, we ought to leave it. If the Old Bill come we can't get out, can we? They'll be all round the gate."

Arnold said, "We don't have to use the gate, do we?" And he nodded to the fence. It had a gap in it, hidden from the gate by the great heap of car bodies. Two planks missing. "We nip through there, scarper along the towpath."

He had spotted his potential escape route long ago. To use it would mean leaving the car; but a car may stand in a garage forecourt through Sunday without pointing to nefarious enterprise, so long as the owner is not caught fiddling about on the premises. A phone call on Monday gets it moved in for a service, and it can be collected on, say, the Thursday. The fuzz may ask questions, but everything is legal and aboveboard. And the garage staff will testify to the fact, if he is a regular customer. As Collie was, and all Vennor's associates, himself included. He gave them special rates. It all helps.

"What about the car?" asked Collie.

Arnold had no time to explain. His nerves, too, were slipping. "For Christ's sake," he snapped, "stop arguing. All right, it's not here. Let's get out of it."

"That's what I been saying all along," Collie said. "Fucking stupid."

They turned, to walk out from behind the stack. It would have been better for Collie had he not caught his foot in a stray leaf-spring unit left lying around. He had to stop, and bend, and fiddle to disengage; which allowed Arnold to draw ahead to where he stopped, stiffened, and said, "Christ!" Because:

He came into the open with his eyes on the stack, hoping with no real hope that he might yet spot that bloody Hillman. His ears heard a sort of tocking; and when he shot to eyes-front, there were three big men, one of them crouched and, without doubt, tapping his knuckles against the petrol tank of one of the in-for-service cars on the concrete; the others upright, one watching the tapper and one looking straight at him, Arnold. It froze him in his tracks. He thought: They're here. The fuzz. And they know. Oh, Jesus.

Collie did not even stop to think, when Arnold said Christ. A red sign flashed up in his mind, lurid as Las Vegas neon. FUZZ! it screamed. FUZZ! FUZZ! He did not so much as see them, any more than they saw him. Hidden by the carcasses, he bent double and took off, over the ten yards between here and that gap in the fence.

How was he to know that all the recent normal heavy rain had collapsed about three feet of the towpath into the swollen canal? Nobody knew it, hardly anybody ever goes along that way. Nothing there but a crummy old warehouse and the back fence of a scrapyard.

If Arnold heard the splash it did not impinge. Mouth dropped open, he was fixated upon the man looking this way, who spoke without moving his eyes. It was

Georgie, and all he said was: "Aye-up." This was enough to turn Hagger, the man watching the tocking, and Charles, who was doing it. They all looked at Arnold.

It is a common phenomenon that people expecting bogeymen believe, at times like this, that they have arrived. Hagger murmured, "Steady. Steady," and moved forward, carefully casual. His henchmen, by no means novices, followed a step behind. In the light coats worn over their smart suits they might well have been policemen, although only graft brings the policemen such quality. But Arnold was not feeling lapels, he was standing stock-still.

Hagger spoke smilingly when he came close, using a friendly tone. "Good afternoon. Looking for spares?"

Now this is just the sort of gambit witty policemen use to open proceedings. Patrol men stopping you for speeding say: I presume your wife is having a baby, sir. "Mm-rrmph," said Arnold. "Mm."

Not very big, if he's pig, Hagger was thinking. But then, the day of the towering policeman is gone. Some, these days, are relatively dwarfish. He kept the frank and friendly smile going. "I don't suppose you know if that car is for sale? The one we were looking at."

Cunning. They're dead cunning, thought Arnold. And where's Collie? "Rrrm," he said. "No. I—er—no." Tough-looking bastards, they were, in spite of the happy smile. Neither of the others wore a smile. One of them was moving around, to look behind the stack. They weren't local, he didn't know them. City?

"Ah," said Hagger. "Well—it doesn't matter. On your own, are you?" Because I'm not sure. Are you pig? If so, there ought to be more.

"Er—mm," said Arnold. Where *was* Collie, then? Still behind the stack? "Er—uh-huh." Or gone, along the towpath?

Charles, having surveyed the ground behind the heap, stepped back; shook his head slightly at his leader, who flickered an eyebrow. Very rarely does a pig venture forth on this sort of caper alone. There should be at least two.

Arnold was also having thoughts. It is true that you can take three of your average plainclothes policemen, three of your average thugs, swap them about, and few will know which is which. But the clothes—the quality, the fit . . . Maybe they weren't Old Bill, maybe they were . . . the geezers Collie said tried to visit Vennor. The thought brought no comfort.

And Hagger was thinking: Something funny here. The man's demeanor doesn't smack of pig. He's scared. And there are no spares on cars stripped down for crushing. Nor was he dressed for poking around in oily places. He said, quite gently, "I think we'd better have a word. In the car."

"Ah-hrrm," said Arnold.

The leader turned away. His minions moved to either side of Arnold, looming large. "Less go," said Georgie, briefly.

They left the heap of carcasses, moving toward the gate; while under the dark and scummy water of the canal Collie choked to death. When that little bit of towpath collapsed, it took with it two of the upright concrete slabs used to retain the bank. Going through the gap bent double, to avoid the horizontal timber bracing halfway up the fence, he went in head first. Smashed his skull on one of the slabs and the last thing he knew was a flash of white light and stars before the eyes. No pain, you'll be glad to hear.

Not all that far away in the town police station, Sergeant Barney Dancey had deserted his little glasshouse for a while to go and rap with gardener's knuckles on the door of the office containing Detective Chief Superintendent (Percy) Fillimore. Invited by that worthy man, he entered carrying a buff envelope. "Thought you ought to see this," he said.

"What is it?" Percy asked. He was having a decent Sunday. Busy; but better than home with the wife.

"Personal effects," said Barney. "Young herbert, name of William Purvis. High on glue." He shook the envelope contents onto the blotter.

"Sniffing? That's not an offense." Percy eyed with distaste the grubby little collection on his desk, which included a crisps bag (barbecued onion flavor) containing a generous dollop, and the tube of Stix Owt from which it was squeezed. Some kind of plastic bag concentrates the fume wonderfully.

Barney did not point out that he knew bloody well it was not an offense. He knew Percy and his odd little ways. He picked up a locket and presented it. "This is the thing," he said.

"Uh-huh." Percy waited for more, turning the locket about, eyeing it narrowly. Not from intent, but because he had these narrow eyes.

"Benjamin Holness. His sister said there was a locket he usually wore." He'd seen her statement. Not much slipped past Barney.

"Plenty of adolescents wear lockets." And earrings, and other jewelry, and water waves. Makeup, too, some of 'em, and not the girls. Bring back National Service. Bring back the cat. Bring back hanging.

"Not with pictures of black girls in them," said Barney. "Not if they're white lads."

Percy opened the locket. "Ah," he said. "Mm. Where is this—this—er . . . ?"

"Purvis. William David Purvis. We've got him downstairs. Disturbing the peace, obstructing. He's still high."

"Mm. Hmm. Right. Is Inspector Cruse in?" Percy was one of the few people who never referred to Cruse as Young Alec.

"Out. Working on the Holness job."

"Raise him, will you? I presume he has his personal radio?"

How would Barney know? But he was a man very slow to umbrage. "Right," he said. "I'll leave the gear with you." Away he went to the radio room, while Percy picked up his telephone to call the Chief Constable.

11

Detective Inspector Rosher worried a little, on his way to Arnold's house. Not about that man, his probable involvement in a nicked-car racket; not about his own pottery leg, the ache in his ribs, the problems created and about to be created by his truncated mobility; but about the cost of this jaunt in a taxi.

An expensive business, nowadays. He was reasonably confident, since expense accounts did not go to Percy, that so long as a well-doctored chit was presented, the taxpayer would swallow the hospital-to-home journey. But a detour comes extra; and the clock ticks inexorably if you tell the driver to wait while you conduct your business.

It would go bitterly against the practice and principle of a lifetime if he had to stand it, or any part of it, himself. Such a thing had never happened before. His ingrained and notorious frugality revolted at the thought of it.

Wherefore he sat frowning as the taxi bowled along. He had not, as yet, put in for refund on the return half of his ticket to London. That would pay for it. But this was a separate item, a perk upon which he had anticipated clear profit. Sod it, when a man plunges out of the sky for it and ends up with a broken ankle and whatnot, he has earned a little something the hard way.

Trouble was, he could not put it down as expense incurred in the course of duty. Presumably he was on sick leave. And probably would collect a finger-wigging for discharging himself from the hospital.

In view of which: best, perhaps, to swallow it. The finger, having wigged, might move on to pick up the chit between itself and the thumb, adding supplementary digits to tear it up small.

No—better not to press. Not just now. Claim for the rail fare, and leave it at that. At least he didn't have to sit fuming in traffic jams, watching the score mount up. Not much traffic about, on a Sunday. And he'd pay the cab off. Arnold could give him a lift home, and no argument. If for some reason he was not available, he could crutch the hundred yards from the house to the main road. Summon a cab from a call box, if he didn't find one cruising.

Here was Arnold's road. The driver spoke over his shoulder. "Which one, Mr. Rosher?"

A small surprise touched the inspector when the man used his name. Had he knocked him, at some time? Possibly, he'd knocked a lot of people. "Keep going," he said. "I'll tell you when we get there." And a few seconds later: "Right."

The driver made no move to help as his client maneuvered heavy leg, crutches, and solid-bodied self out onto the pavement. In the time of fumbling for money, he said, "When you coming on telly again? I saw you when you copped the Avenger."

It pleased Rosher, always, when people remembered his moments of glory. Well, it pleases anybody. He handed over his money, stretching leather lips into grim joviality. "When they offer me a contract."

The driver looked hard at his meager tip. "Ought to put you on with Morecambe and Wise," he said. "You're a bloody sight funnier." And he drove away.

With difficulty, because of the crutches under his arms, Rosher resettled the black hat low upon his simian brow. Then he turned to Arnold's quite presentable house, crutched up the short drive, and rang the bell. A clip-clap of heels along the hall and there was Mrs. Gutte, really rather fetching in sort of a tea gown. She bought it in a shop where the background music concentrated on Mantovani.

It was Rosher's habit, when faced with a member of the female public upon her doorstep, to snatch off the black hat and wreath himself in smiles as he mangled vowels into an accent rich and strange. But Arnold Gutte was bent; and no matter how fetching, how lady-like, and—in the days before his trauma-induced impotence—lust-worthy, the wives of the bent are the wives of the bent, and therefore not eligible.

However, he sternly called her madam. "Good afternoon, madam," he said. "Is Arnold in?"

"I'm afraid he's not," she said. Charmingly, but with a slight overhang because a cut off the joint was in the oven, with the Brussels sprouts going brown and the gravy drying up. "Who shall I say was wanting him?" Come on crutches, like a gorilla in a black hat.

"What time are you expecting him back?"

"I'm afraid I don't know. He didn't say." The bastard. Well, he'd get no apple crumble. Not worthy of the name, it had dried into Bath brick.

"Hrrm. Tell him Detective Inspector Rosher called."

"Ah," she said. "Yes. I will." And watching as he humped away without another word, she thought: What's he been up to now? And I wonder how long he'll get for it? Then she went back inside, turned off the gas, and gave his dinner to the dog. She would *not* slave over a hot stove all day. Besides, it was on the cards that he wouldn't need it.

Inspector Rosher reached the street again, swinging now on his crutches. Not handling them yet with the insouciant verve of the true cripple, but beginning to come to grips with the fundamentals of technique. A hundred yards away was the main road. As he turned toward it a car came around the corner, with four men in it. It stopped just across the street from where he stood.

He looked at three of the men, and thought: They're the buggers who visited Vennor. He looked at the other and thought: That's Arnold. And he's sitting in the backseat, between two of the buggers.

There was a short conversation in the car, the man at the wheel turning around to conduct his share. Rosher could see his face clearly. He put it into his mental file. After a moment Arnold Gutte got out, and the car drove away.

Arnold came over; obviously so preoccupied, Rosher knew, that he had not noticed the cripple, or, if he had, certainly had not translated the image into Old Blubbergut. When the inspector hailed him loudly, he could see the man jump from here.

"Hang on, lad," Rosher cried. "I want a word with you."

Short of running—and he looked as though he might—Arnold had no choice. He had to approach, was already doing so because Rosher was almost in front of his house. He said as he came, "Ha! Ha-ah. Mr. Rosher."

"Afternoon, Arnold," said Detective Inspector Rosher. "Who's your friends?"

When they had reached the car, at approximately the time when Collie's soul left the body, rising coughing and spitting from that turgid water, Gentleman Jack Hagger got into the front seat. Georgie and Charles urged Arnold into the back and climbed in after, one on each side. Hagger, twisted around, said, over the backseat, and still rather gently, "Are you a friend of Mr. Vennor?"

Now, this hoisted Arnold onto the horns. Should he

say yes, or should he say no? If they *were* Old Bill—which they weren't; or were they?—to say yes could have him in for questioning. If they were not Old Bill—if they were another mob, say, got wind—no or yes could be equally perilous. "Er—mm," he said. "That is—no. Er—not really."

No, Hagger told himself: not fuzz. He said, "We thought at first you were pig. You're not, I suppose?"

"Ha ha," said Arnold. "Ha ha ha." So *they* weren't pig. "No. Not pi . . . Who—who—who—?"

The matter had to be pressed home, and Hagger was no fool. If the man wasn't fuzz, he certainly was not an innocent bystander. Wouldn't have entered the car so meekly, would not have been so guiltily nervous sitting in it. "Are you by any chance," he asked, "one of Vennor's boys?"

"V-v-vennor's boys?"

That was it. That's what he was. Look at him, shitting himself. "You don't have to worry—you're among friends."

"F-f-friends?"

"We're the London end."

"L-l-london end?"

"We didden oughta be sitting abaht 'ere," said Georgie. "We oughta move on." He was right, of course. It was no place to sit chatting.

Hagger twisted the ignition key. "I expect you have things to tell us that we ought to know." The car began to move, leaving Collie's vehicle alone by the pumps.

"I don't—I don't—I don't know—nothing—about—nothing."

"We can always shoot yer kneecaps orf," said Georgie. And Hagger reproved him at once. Still speaking gently.

"Now, that's no way to talk. No violence, between friends."

They did not drive far. No need to. Arnold had known there was a London end—the guard in the truck, lads on the raid—and the clothes on these men, the accents, the ambience, all said London. They frightened him; and God knows, he had been nervous enough already, except for the brief interlude when leadership went to his adrenaline. Hagger said, "You want proof, of course"; and he spelled out the raid: the plan and its execution, exactly as it happened. Even then—after all, a lot was up for grabs—Arnold said, "How do I know you're not—not—pigs. Or something."

Now they frightened him even more. Hagger said, "Show him your shooters, lads"; and the other men reached under their arms. "See?" the leader said, without looking around. "Lugers. The pigs don't use Lugers, do they? All right, put 'em away."

From here, Arnold answered questions. He'd carried guns himself, on several jobs in the past; but a sawn-off shotgun usually, and never with truly evil intent. It was a protective measure, a frightener. But these bastards looked as if they shot their own breakfast, and didn't care if it was their aged grandma.

At length, as they cruised near to Arnold's home, Hagger said, "So. We know there's a jalopy. We know it's a blue Hillman. We know the gear's on board. We know there are two herberts, but we don't know who they are or how to get at them. And we don't know where the jalopy is. Right?"

"That's right," said Arnold. Put like that, it sounded a right cockup. Charles said as much. He said, "Right cockup."

"Poor organization." Hagger spoke more to emphasize his own eminent capacity rather than in criticism of Vennor, who really had done rather well, for a turnip nosher from the sticks. Played it all very close. Hagger approved that. But then the silly bugger hit a truck. "How many of you did you say there are?"

"Four," Arnold said. Plonker, Ratface, Collie, and himself. And, of course, the two herberts. "And the two herberts," he added.

"Call them together," Hagger commanded. "First thing to do is find those two. We'll run you home, you get on the blower. We'll find a hotel. In the city." Not here. Small-town people might notice three sharp men with the urban look. "I'll ring you as soon as we're settled, you fix a meeting. Soon as possible. Let's have your phone number."

Arnold directed the car to his street, and none of the occupants took particular note of the cripple on crutches. Arnold, utterly churned up, did not even see him. Hagger said, "Right. Stay in and wait for my call. And tell your mates to stand by. And listen, sonny —no monkey business. When you play with us, you're up in the first division."

So Arnold got out, the car drove away, and as he crossed the street to his house, the cripple cried out, "Hang on, lad—I want a word with you."

Arnold's head jerked, and he felt himself leave the pavement. Rosher! Bloody Rosher! Last heard of in hospital, flat on his back. His feet came down angled, all set to turn and run him away, in a small cloud of dust and a smell of skreeking rubber where he vanished around the corner. But he couldn't do that. Fatal. He forced the feet onward, saying, "Ha! Ha-ah. Mr. Rosher."

"Afternoon, Arnold," said Detective Inspector Rosher. "Who's your friends?"

"Friends?" Arnold said. There was a tremble in it, a touch of squeakiness. "Friends? Oh—*them*. Yes. Just—some—fellers I know."

"Friends of one Elton Vennor?"

The bastard was using the sort of tone a jocular snake might use to a baby rabbit. He normally did, when he spoke to the likes of Arnold. "Elton Vennor? Who's Elton Vennor?" And then, remembering that Collie said the bastard saw him, Arnold, at the hospital last night: "Oh—Elton *Vennor*. Yes. No. I—er— no. They're—business associates."

"That damns 'em, Arnold, doesn't it? Any business associate of yours has got to be bent."

"Ha ha ha, Mr. Rosher," Arnold said. "You will have your little joke."

Rosher's brownstone teeth were glimmering dully, the leather face seamed in grim joviality under the black hat. He hitched on his crutches. "You ought to hear me in court," he said. "But then, of course, you have."

"Long time ago now, though, Mr. Rosher." Arnold hated, as all the little bent do faced with such confrontations, the ingratiating smile that he felt puckering his face, the close-to-a-whine tone thinning his vocal chords. "Ain't it?"

"Never mind, lad, you could be hearing it again soon. Got a little something going on, have we?"

"There you go again, Mr. Rosher. Great sense of humor." Like a gorilla, sadistically tearing the skin off terrified bananas.

"Something in the motor car line, is it? You and Collie? And your friends? And Mr. Vennor?"

Oh, Christ! The bastard was on. How, for Christ's sake? He'd been, Collie said, stuck there with his leg in the air. "What are you talking about?" Arnold was puckered in that ingratiating smile right up to the hairline. "I don't know what you're talking about."

"You will, lad, you will," the terrible bastard said, "when I get my hand in your collar. Where's Collie? Out nicking another motor, is he?"

"I don't know, do I? I mean—I'm just going to have my dinner, ain't I? I mean—I haven't seen him, have I? Not for a long time."

"I have." The teeth reappeared, big and brown like menacing cough lozenges. "This morning. Tell him I was asking after his health, he looked very green. Where's your car?"

"Car?"

"You can run me home, seeing I've taken all the

trouble to call on you." And that takes care of the taxi fare.

"Ah." Where was his car? Oh, Christ—still at Bishop Adam Park, where he left it. "Yes. Well—it's not here."

"Not here? Don't tell me somebody whipped it. That'd be ironic, wouldn't it, under the present circumstances?"

"It's—er—it's in."

"In?"

"For servicing. That's why the—the fellers gave me a lift home. From the pub."

"Pubs are closed, lad. Have been for a long time."

"Mm. We went for a meal. After." I should have got 'em to put me down in the main road, out of sight. But how was I to know?

"In at Vennor's, is it? The car."

"No. No—it's at Higgis's. Just round the corner. I—er—I have to go, Mr. Rosher. The wife. Been nice talking to you."

"I'm glad you've enjoyed it, Arnold. I wish I could say the same." Let the little sod go. Nothing to do him for, at this stage. He knows his rights, and he'll use 'em, if you press. And you've scared the shit out of him. "Enjoy your dinner, then. I just met the missus, poor lady. And do me a favor? Ring for a taxi, when you get in. I'll be waiting for it on the corner."

Arnold hurried away. As he opened his door, the inspector called again. "Arnold."

"Yes, Mr. Rosher?"

"You haven't even asked how I am."

"Ah. Yes. How—how are you?"

"I'm not going to tell you now, because I don't believe you really care."

Under the hat the terrible choppers glinted back the light, brownly. In like a bum-shot bunny went Arnold, and shut out the evil sight.

It was late afternoon before Billy Purvis came down from his high to where he might be expected to make sense if he was interviewed. The chief constable, summoned to the telephone by his wife from the basement where he made his own wine, felt that there was no real need for a personal appearance. In accordance with his belief that a force works best when treated with kindness and an abundance of encouragement—his predecessor believed in a boot up its arse—he complimented Percy upon the good work that brought, it looked like, retribution to yet another client; and Percy accepted the approval without feeling the need to mention that all he had been doing was sitting at his desk, while two common coppers ran the bugger in and Barney Dancey noticed the locket.

He went down to the underground cells with Detective Inspector Young Alec Cruse, called back from his sniffing around the haunts where young herberts congregate, and found Billy surly and still dazed in aftermath. The hangover from glue is every bit as draconian as the grim letdown from liquor. The young man sat hunched on the edge of the cell bunk, very sick.

Percy went straight in. No preliminary courtesies. He displayed the locket and snapped, "All right, lad. Where did you get this?"

Billy blinked, trying to bring the object into focus. "What is it?" he muttered.

"It's a locket, matching the description of one missing from the person of Benjamin Holness, found murdered. I should like to know how you account for its being among your personal effects."

Billy's eyes came up from the locket, sharpened abruptly with shock. Truth is, he had forgotten all about the colored boy. He'd read no papers, he had no idea the lad was dead. "I—don't know nothing about no—" he said. Not muttering now.

Percy snapped in. Whatever was said about Percy, and many said much, nobody could fault him as an interrogator. He could wheedle, he could caress, he could browbeat; and when he snapped, it came like the crack of an iced knout. "Lying won't help you, lad. Don't make me get nasty." Unobtrusively, Young Alec Cruse produced his little black book.

"I don't know nothing about nothing," said big Billy Purvis. The locket. The fucking locket. Not worth a fucking light, he hadn't even looked at it since he took it. Dead? How could he be dead, he only got hit once.

"All right, lad, if that's the way you want it. You don't have to answer questions, but I must warn you that should you wish to say anything, anything you do say will be taken down and may be used in evidence."

"I don't know nothing," Billy said; reverted to muttering, and now with a note of panic in it.

At this very moment Gentleman Jack Hagger and party were meeting for the first time with the party of whom, like it or not (and he liked it less, now, with every passing moment) Arnold Gutte found himself willy-nilly leader.

When he got into his house—and his wife had vanished into her kitchen because she had no wish to be involved—he dialed Collie's number straight away. But Collie was not there. So he rang Ratface Rorke. Not that Ratface was a man to be leaned upon in time of trouble; but sod it, he was embroiled, and Arnold needed to share his burden. And he had to call the lads together. He said, "Listen—three geezers—big geezers—from London. Working with Vennor—they put the guard in and that. They're here. They've got fucking Lugers. And Rosher's out."

"He's what?" said Ratface. The alarm showed in his voice. That name had effect, even upon a man who did not know he was in.

So Arnold told him again, and went on to sketch, very briefly, the upsetting happenings. When he finished, Ratface said, "Where's Collie and Plonker, then?"

"Collie ain't back yet, I tried his number. Plonker's mum and dad'll be there, I didn't want to have to flannel 'em before I could get at him. Listen—I'm getting off this blower." Never talk too much on the telephones.

"We oughta meet, before we meet these geezers."

"I can't get out, I've got to wait for 'em to call." They'll have my guts, else. Why—oh, why did I let 'em know where I live? Because I was too shook up to think straight, that's why. "Listen—I'll ring you back. When they've rung. You ring the others, tell 'em to stand by. Then when I ring you back, you ring 'em back." And he hung up, leaving Ratface to work that out.

Hagger called nearly an hour later, by which time Arnold had sat down to, but had not eaten, a small omelet cooked up by his wife in lieu of dinner, which the dog had eaten with relish despite the dried-up gravy. By the time he'd golloped the greater part of that omelet, that dog thought it was Christmas. Because all this came in addition to his Yummy-Chum.

The telephone said when Arnold clapped it to his ear and spoke his name, "Your friends here. You know the Empress Hotel?"

"Yes," said Arnold. Of course he knew it. Great, monstrous pile of glass and varicolored concrete twenty stories high, dominating the city center. Everybody knew it.

"Ask for Mr. Smith. Soon."

"I thought we were meeting here—"

"Never mind that. Do as you're told." The phone went dead. Hagger had decided: safer in the city.

Now, in the late afternoon, Ratface's car nosed into the city and headed for the Empress Hotel. Nobody had to direct the owner/driver, he knew the way. Seated beside him was Arnold, his car to be collected on the way back. He was wondering whether Collie had returned, to remove his vehicle from Vennor's forecourt. If so: where had he gone in it?

"Funny about Collie," he remarked as they drove toward the city center. "You'd have thought he'd have gone straight home." He was missing Collie. For years they'd worked elbow to elbow. It increased Arnold's nervousness, not to have him here.

"Wouldn't have scarpered, would he?" Plonker wondered, from the backseat.

"No. No, he wouldn't do that." Or would he? Yes, he would. "That's the Empress, over there."

"I know, I know," snapped Ratface. He, too, was under tension.

No more was said while they drew up in front of the great hotel and a man in a green uniform stepped forward to open the car doors. They went on into the reception hall, all carpeted and chandeliered. Here Arnold asked for Mr. Smith, and they were whisked upward in a neat and purring elevator. Hagger and Co. awaited them, too big and solid for a suite intended for quivering brides. Hagger was a man who demanded the best. He said, "Come in. Introduce your friends."

"Yes," said Arnold. "Mr. Rorke. And—er—Mr. Milgrave." He said nothing about the missing Collie.

"How do you do," Hagger said. "I'm Smith. This is Mr. Brown, and that's Mr. Green. Now then—about our little problem. Sit down, there are no fleas."

Fifteen minutes later the *tout ensemble* stepped into that purring elevator and were cosseted down to the reception floor. They stepped into a fading fag-end of a gray day, where the green man ushered the town boys obsequiously into Ratface's car and stood back calling them tight-fisted bastards under his breath as they made no effort to press something that folded into his gloved and willing hand. The London men crossed to Hagger's car, in the parking bay. They drove away in convoy, and Plonker said, "All very well, looking in all the discos and that, but there's only four of us. *If* Collie ain't scarpered. And what about Rosher? Bastard, he is."

The only answer he got from Arnold was a grunt. He had already pointed out these problems when Smith— Smith? Brown? Green? Not bloody likely—directed that the town discothèques, slot-machine arcades, and the like be scoured in search of the two tearaways. The hard man had fixed him with a cold eye and snapped, "Have to hop about a bit, then, won't you?"

Oh, hard men. They scared Arnold. They scared Plonker and Ratface, too. Particularly when the subject of Rosher came under review.

Arnold had to mention him. Hagger said at once, "Rosher? Who's Rosher?" So Arnold told him. Said he was a bastard, Plonker and Ratface agreeing fervently. Told of Rosher's sudden materialization, sprung from his sickbed like a Demon King on crutches. Said that he, Arnold, feared from his, Rosher's, conversation that he, Rosher, was on; although the bastard seemed to believe that he, Arnold, was engaged in a car caper with Mr. Vennor. Did not mention that discussion of the matter in the car coming over had brought all three participants to the verge of mass scarper. But it was enormous tickle; and the men commanding their presence were London, with London know-how—and maybe a tail on them. So here they were; and wishing more than ever that they were not as Smith said, "Mm. Let's have his address."

"What for?" said Arnold.

"We may have to visit him."

"Visit him? Why?"

Georgie spoke up. "We might 'ave to blow him away."

Then again: Listen to this. Upon the subject of Vennor. "If we can't get hold of these lads of yours, we'll

have to think about getting to Vennor. You keep ringing the hospital. As soon as he can speak, we might
have to get him out of there."

Arnold: "Get him out?"

Smith (with nasty smile, shared by Brown and
Green): "Go and collect him. All you have to do is map
us the layout of the hospital."

Three hard men with Lugers. From the big league,
from London. No wonder the lowly division men drove
back to the town in near-silence, each biting his mental nails and one (it was Plonker) his physical ones, to
the very quick. And to crown this jolly day: they went
from disco to amusement arcade, pub to coffee bar, and
back again, all evening around the town center, separately sheep-dogged by those big men. Completely use-
less exercise, had they but known it. Billy was in the
police cells, and Mike by now in the cottage hospital.
And Collie didn't turn up.

This the local lads knew now, regarding the London
men: with all that tickle at stake, they'd not be moving
out with a pebble left unturned.

12

By the time the two cars reached town, Billy Purvis had admitted that he was in the town center on Friday night, but denied knowledge of any incident involving a black boy. He'd visited the Devil's Den disco, he said, and then the Unicorn public house for a few drinks; returning afterward to the disco, where he stayed until it closed. He agreed that the short route to his home led through Wallace Street and that he normally used it, but said that on Friday he went the long way around, through the shopping center. Sweating with fear, he said he had friends who could prove it; and pressed, he passed on to panic and blurted the name of Mike Gibbins.

"And where does this friend live?" Percy asked, while Young Alec Cruse poised the ball-point over his notebook.

So when evening came glumly to end this gray day, six villains were not the only people seeking Mike Gibbins. Inspector Cruse took a sergeant, and they visited Mike's home, where his gray-haired, obstreperously sluttish mother (his father was already gone drinking) said that he'd gone out this morning and hadn't been home since. No, she didn't know where he'd gone. With that Billy Purvis, she expected. What did they want him for, he hadn't done nothing. Had he?

No need for emergency action, then, at this stage. Cruse left his sergeant standing about, to intercept the young man when and if he came home. He used his radio to report the position and to ask for a call to be put out to all personnel, requesting that they keep an open eye. Then he drove down to the town center, to check the veracity—if anybody remembered seeing him—of Billy's statement regarding his movements on Friday night. And, of course, to gather Mike Gibbins if he was there.

His business at the town center did not take long. The lads had been together, they said so at pub and disco both. Which meant that unless they went home separately, Mike's involvement equaled Billy's. And Billy's involvement was deep.

A pity, really, that Cruse's inquiries went so smoothly. He returned to his car, suggested through his radio link with the station that the picking up of Mike Gibbins be treated now as a matter of urgency, and drove away. Back to the station. When a case is moving, a detective does not go home. It contributes no end to their marital problems. Of which, God knows, they have many.

Had he been delayed, by just two or three minutes, he might well have observed the arrival in the town square of six men, three known to him as bent and three big, snappy strangers, who separated into pairs and began to peer into places where grown men never go. And being a young, keen, and intelligent officer, very certainly he would have moved unobtrusively from doorway to doorway, keeping watch and wondering. Couldn't have watched them all; but he would have been around when they all met up again later for a brief conference before the strangers drove away, leaving the known bent murmuring together around their car.

What had happened to Mike Gibbins? Well:

When he drove rapidly away from where two police-men loaded Billy into a panda car, he acted in obedi-ence to the instinct that bristles the hair of the natur-ally bent when they see Old Bill and a bosom friend engaged in professional intercourse, and urges flight. By the time he crossed the town center, his mind had simmered down to a mixture of trepidation and anger.

Anger against Billy. The twat. What had he done a bloody stupid thing like that for?

Because he *was* bloody stupid, that's why.

Well, they couldn't knock him for sniffing. They'd have to let him go. But—you couldn't know, could you, what he'd tell 'em while he was high?

Sod him, the big, stupid berk.

They might keep him in. Disturbing the peace. Tak-ing a chop at the coppers, maybe—he liked to have a go, Billy did, when he was high or a bit pissed.

He'd looked as though they'd belted him.

Good job he, Mike, as brain of the outfit, was holding the Vennor money. If the prat hadn't slung it all up in the air like confetti when he was high, the fuzz would have dropped very heavy when they found his half on him.

It was not the business of the black boy that worried Mike. He did not even think about it. No reason to, so far as he was concerned it was merely a minor incident with a few beers taken, a blurred recollection from an evening that was blurred. What did worry him was the Vennor job, and various little fiddles all shared with Billy. Like the car he was driving. All right for five hundred miles, they'd tarted it up well; but you wouldn't want the fuzz running a hard rule over it. Not when you've been knocked once for flogging an unroadworthy.

The thing to do, he told himself, is to carry on as normal. You can't go and get him out. Probably by this evening they'll have sprung him. He might even roll up at the track. What time he comes out of it depends on how high he was.

Mike drove on, and spent the rest of the morning doing business with the punter buying the car; sitting in the passenger seat while the man tasted it along the bypass, skirting the lay-bys where the armed raid took place; and haggling the price, which showed a handsome profit when all was done, paid for in cash.

From here he went to a café for a meal, with chips. Too early to expect that Billy might appear, but he used the one they always patronized before afternoon meetings at the track. Their car was there already. They had use of a shed right on the track perimeter. For a few shillings a week they kept the souped-up, crash-barred, largely homemade article off the road, under cover and very handy for local events and practice sessions.

Fed, he got to the track early and spent the time until half past two doing what he loved to do: tinkering with the engine, delicately adjusting, listening with talented ear to its note; seeking perfection. Told that he was making an act of unknowing worship, an instinctive obeisance to a God of perfection, he would have said bollicks.

As he worked, he fretted; but immersion in vocation soothes wonderfully. By the time the meeting started, he felt only the familiar joyful adrenaline flow.

In one way, it suited him not to have Billy here. It meant he could drive every race for which they had entered, where normally they shared the rides between them. By the halfway interval, he had won two and gained a second place. All cash prizes, and not a dent on the car. Well, no fresh ones. Stock cars are never without, denting is what the game thrives on.

He was not engaged in the second heat after the interval. He stood leaning against the wire fence of the pit area, at ease now and totally absorbed. Sod Billy. Sod 'em all. This was his hallowed land, here all his scattered bits came together. Here was applause, and the respect of fellowmen of like mind.

The heat finished. Tommy Harman, who won after a battering, came motoring toward the pits; and Mike saw the flames come from under the battered, long bonnet hiding a wildly oversized engine.

One of the attributes of talent akin to genius: it sees in a flash the overall picture, complete before it exists. Mike saw the fuel pipe, not properly attached after tinkering, perhaps, shaken from the carburetor by the battering; the manifold directly beneath, red-hot now after hard races. The sudden flashback through fuel system to tank. Boom!

He saw something else, too. Tommy knew—but he couldn't get out. He was struggling with the clasp of his safety belt. Hands fumbling in sudden panic snarl them up, sometimes.

Mike was running. And give the boy full credit: he knew what was liable to happen. But he ran, and straightened the twisted belt; and he even shoved Tommy clear ahead of himself. But that damned safety belt—he caught his foot in it and was checked, just when the flashback set the bomb off.

He was very lucky, really. His head was away and he was nearly clear; but the flames took him in the legs. He staggered and fell with his overalls on fire. It was Tommy who beat out the flames, before the St. John's ambulance men could move. That cash money in the lad's pocket charred badly.

They took him to St. Barnolph's. Where else? As the ambulance moved away, the policeman on duty took out his notebook and said to the promoter, "What's the boy called?"

Now, for professional purposes, Mike long ago abandoned his own surname. "Gibbins" lacks charisma. He adopted instead the name of a legendary racing driver, idol of his boyhood. His slummy bedroom at home was plastered with pictures of the man.

"Mike," the promoter said. "Michael Stewart."

13

Many interesting things happened next day. For one, start of work at Vennor's garage was delayed by the double excitements of the boss's crash and serious condition, and the fishing out of a body from the canal beyond the scrapyard fence, discovered by a bus conductor having his day off and on the way to early morning fishing. The item of a car left untended at the pumps ranked small beside these things. It was driven around to the concrete area, to await explanation from an owner who would arrive to tell why he left it there.

It was after nine o'clock, when the office girl and a lizardlike man who lurked in the showroom arrived together, before the manager said, "Well—come on, then. Let's get a little work done, shall we?"

The typewriter was unwrapped, the lizard-like man flicked a duster over a wing mirror or two, mechanics began to borrow one another's tools; and out among the oily wastes the boy Albert was raked down off the fence (he had mounted and was hung over it looking for clues, or coppers, or corpses, or anything else that would lighten the burden of the day) and sent to his position, ready to guide the great magnets into close contact with the scrap bodies when Sam Godwin, who mounted now into his crane, lowered them down; before raising them again to swing yet another body across into the crusher watched over by Old Bob, who had a wobbly eye.

Another thing that happened: Detective Inspector Rosher had a visitor to his home, and this was a very rare occurrence. He had managed to wash and shave, and to assemble eggs and a rasher of bacon, and to fry them. Not easy, on those crutches, but he did it. He even made tea, black and biting; and as he was settling to breakfast at the cluttered table in his cluttered kitchen, the front doorbell rang.

"Sod it," he said, and got up to crutch his way through a living room that would have reduced his fat wife to tears, if she had any left, and across the hall where a mighty cobweb had grown, he noticed, between the ceiling and the top of the dusty lampshade. He opened the door; and there on the step, a small car on his drive behind her, stood Nurse Holness. He said, "Ah. Mmm."

"Good morning." Her smile came a trifle lopsided. And it was not a bad morning. Bright intervals, the weatherman said. Rain later. "Is this where it's all at?"

"Morning," he said. "What—er—?"

"Thought I'd just look you up."

"Ah." He hesitated a moment; levered himself back from the door. "Well—come in. Come in."

"Thank you." She stepped inside, dark eyes automatically taking in the dustiness, the generally seedy air that had spread by now to the hall. "Just come off duty. Day off, and I go on days. I was a bit bothered, you shouldn't have discharged yourself. You got a bump on the head."

"I'm all right."

"That's what they all say. Then they drops dead."

"Go through," he said. "I'm in the kitchen. Having breakfast."

God, she thought as they went through the living room into the kitchen, he needs a woman, or something. Look at the state of the cooker. He spoke again. "Like a cup of tea?"

"Sure," she said. "Just what I need." And as he set himself to crutch to the cooker, where the kettle steamed on a low gas, "Why don't I get it? I'm not on no crutches. Sit down—cold eggs and bacon don't do no good to a body. Where do you keep the cups?"

"In the cupboard." He sat down at the table; picked up his knife and fork. His tea mug steamed like a wicked little cauldron.

She opened the kitchen cabinet. Two saucepans fell out. She stuffed them back and selected a cup. It left a ring on the shelf. "Matron'd have a fit if she saw this lot. I had a call from your Inspector Cruse. About Benjie. They're questioning somebody. He'd got his locket."

"When was this?" He asked it with immediate professional interest, through eggs and bacon. Both congealing, but his domestic circumstances had brought him to stoicism in such matters. If he hadn't burned everything black, it was a good breakfast.

"Last night. He rang the hospital, last night. They found the feller yesterday."

"Hrrrmph. Good." Was that why she came? Thinking she might gather inside information? "Thought it wouldn't be long."

"We can't have it yet. The locket. They need it as evidence." Talking, she poured tea from his pot; boggled at its venomous glowering and diluted it well with water from the kettle. The smile she made now quivered a little. But she said, brightly, "Well—how you making out?"

"No grumbles. Bit awkward, hobbling about on crutches."

"Well, it's your own fault. Looks like you don't do much housework anytime."

He bridled. "I get by."

"Doesn't look like it." She put the tea aside on his

stained draining board. A sip had been enough. "You've got to go back to the hospital today. Right? Get your head looked at. Can't drive or nothing, can you?"

"There're taxis."

"Thought I might run you down, wangle priority. You can't do *that* for yourself."

"Ah. Thank you." That was nice of her. He inserted a mouthful of breakfast and mangled it between his big brown grinders. Picked up his mug of baleful brew.

"There's your telephone," she said.

He'd heard it. Almost, he snapped: I'm not bloody deaf. He put his mug down and seized his crutches, to hobble through to the living room.

It was Sergeant Barney Dancey. He said, "Alf? Morning. How's things? Good, we heard you'd liberated yourself. Couple of things I thought you might like to hear about. Your nurse's brother—we've got a lad. Had his locket among his gear."

"Uh-huh." Don't say you know, it'll mean making explanations. And you know what they'll say, if it gets around that you've got a bird up here. They'll say you're at it again. "Who have you got?"

"Lad called Billy Purvis—you did him once, car caper."

"Ah. Purvis ... Purvis ... had a mate ... " Rosher never forgot a client, or anything about him. "Gibbins. Name of Gibbins. They rigged a banger."

"Michael Gibbins. We've got a call out for him. And another old mate of yours. Cauliflower Davis. Fished him out of the canal this morning, back of Vennor's garage."

"Dead?"

"Not half."

"Done?"

"No. We don't think so—Ted Hocking's been on it, reckons he missed his footing coming through the fence from the scrapyard. The towpath's washed away right there."

"Well, well." Well, well. Cauliflower Davis. Arnold Gutte's mate. Visitors both to Vennor, in hospital. Visitors both to Vennor's scrapyard? After dark? Through a gap in the fence? If not after dark, how do you drown because you put your weight where a chunk of towpath is missing?

"Thought you'd like to know," said Barney, who rang, really, because he had that kindly heart, and thought he'd just bring a little human contact to poor old Alf, stuck up there crippled in an isolation that simply would not suit him, that's all. Nobody else would go near the poor old bugger.

I suppose, Inspector Rosher thought, I'd better start playing it by the book. There's matter should be snuffed at, here. "Is Young Alec about?" he asked.

"Not yet. He was working late. He's in court this morning, reckon he'll go straight there. Back about lunchtime, I expect." Although, as both knew, that would depend upon what time the beak dealt with Cruse's particular felon. "Percy's in his office."

Sod Percy. "Doesn't matter. Thanks, Barney." I can ring Cruse later.

"Any time. Look after yourself." And Barney put the phone down; turned to attend to a Constable Rumbold who had just come in towing a little old tramp, done for trying door handles on parked cars.

Rosher hobbled back to the kitchen. The visitor was washing up. "You're gonna start an outbreak of typhoid or something," she said, "if you don't do something quick."

Once, he would have blasted her. Bloody liberty. But he had learned to take advantage of any small help offered. Not that any ever was, or had been since the departure of a brothel madam who fed him like a king and kept his house like a palace; for a little time before she decamped, the wicked bitch. She still came back, to wander about in his dreams. He said, "Old client of mine, the lad who had your brother's locket. Did him for rigging a car. Him and his mate. There's a call out for the other lad."

"Uh-huh." She stood at the sink with her back toward him, scrubbing among Fairy bubbles; and the quiver that had touched her smile sounded now in her voice as she said, "Better finish your breakfast and give me them plates. Then I'll run you down to the hospital. Get there early, I can get you in quick, no hanging about." Two mugs, three plates, one wire whisk, and a frying pan later, she added, "Don't tell 'em I visited you. It's not really ethical."

Ten minutes later they left the house and he loaded his leg into her little car. She got in beside him and they drove away, a black girl and a grim gorilla in a black hat. She might well have caught him in some jungle and trained him to wear that hat, with a battleship-gray raincoat over a durable blue serge suit.

The sun was shining. On the other side of town the boy Albert positioned the magnets, the man Sam swung car bodies. Old Bob stood wobbling his eye beside his movable-sided crusher, to remove those bodies and stack them on one side when they were reduced to neat, squarish packages. From the main city road, Jack Hagger, with his friends, had just arrived and was turning his car snout in the direction of Bishop Adam Park, where he had arranged to meet Arnold, Plonker, and Ratface, who more than likely, the Hagger party opined, would not be there.

Despite the best endeavors of planning committees, the town still looks very pretty when the sun shines. Inspector Rosher sat in his little seat and frowned silently at it. He was thinking, and this thinking caused him to say, "Are you in a hurry?"

"Not particularly. Why?"

"There's a garage. Vennor's, in Scone Road. I'd like to have a look at it."

"Why?"

Why? Because something funny's on. Hot cars. And I

haven't enough of a case to go snooping direct; but I can call to follow up the Cauliflower Davis caper, and cast an eye about. Never know what'll turn up. But I'd better not tell you that. "Old client of mine, fished out of the canal this morning. I'd like to have a look at where it happened."

"Uh-huh." She drove on, adding after a small silence, "You don't mind being seen with a black girl, then?"

His eyes flickered sideways at her. "Why should I?"

"Some do."

Psychologists and those who knew him might have said that Rosher's mind was of the type from which a classic chauvinism is constructed. They would have been wrong. No credit to him in this, perhaps—truth is, he held his fellow beings in low esteem anyway, white or black or khaki. His sole concern was to keep them in order. So long as they behaved themselves he gave not a damn what color they'd come. In this small town, with its small immigrant population—there were almost none, on his own particular patch—most of the villainy came from whites, if only by virtue of their greater number. So now he grunted, and sat watching the world go by until the car turned into Scone Road, when she said, quietly, "Benjie wouldn't have been dead, if he hadn't been black."

He grunted again. When they reached the garage he said, "Pull into the forecourt."

"Better not be long." She steered the car in. "If we don't get there early you'll have to wait your turn."

He swung his leg out from the car and followed it, while she stood holding his crutches. Then she walked beside him as he heaved his gorilla bulk into the office, where he fixed with a hard little eye a youngish man who had wavy dark hair and an undertaker's moustache, flashed his identity card in its well-pickled wallet, and said, "Morning. Detective Inspector Rosher. Manager about?"

The man wreathed himself swiftly in an ingratiating smile. "Ah," he said. "Good morning. I'm the manager." He was thinking: Sod that stupid bastard. And he meant Collie, who had brought the police here. Very, very few garage men have a completely easy conscience.

"Uh-huh. Understand you had an incident here last night. Man drowned."

"Yes. Mm. That's right."

"I'll have a look around, if it's all right with you." I'll have a look around if it's not all right with you. You're bent for a start, it's all in your eyes.

"Ah. Yes. Er—the scrapyard is this way. . . ." The manager moved forward, toward the door by which they had entered.

"We'll go through the building," the inspector said, and, as the wide grin fluttered a little, "We imagine they—or he—was trespassing with intent. We'll take a look at the locks."

"But he's dead," the manager said.

"Even so." And Rosher set off along the route that would lead through the showroom, and then the workshop, and so out by the back door onto the concrete area fronting the barren earth of the scrapyard.

Nothing to see, really. He had not expected that there would be, nobody in the car-nicking caper displays the loot in his own showroom or leaves it standing around in his workshop. But much can be learned, sometimes, from the demeanor of the man who conducts you through the premises. Watch for the ingratiating smile—particularly accompanied by a little cold sweat.

They emerged onto the concrete, and Rosher pretended to examine the lock, just as the boy Albert squinted past the carcass to which he was attaching the magnets and called up to the man Sam, "There's one 'ere ain't been stripped down."

"Where?" said Sam.

"Under 'ere. Where you bleeding fink?"

"Don't be lippy," Sam advised, "or you'll get me toe up your arse. How many we got before we get to it?"

"Couple more. Both on top."

"Get on with it, then. Get them magnets on."

Magnets positioned, another body swung aloft just as Inspector Rosher turned away from the door and headed out across the open ground. Passing, he ran his eyes over a couple of cars standing innocently on the concrete, one of them belonging to Collie. He said, "Your boss came unstuck, I hear."

"Yes," the manager replied. "Mm. He's in the hospital."

"This young lady works there. No doubt she'll give him your regards."

"He's in Intensive Care, I believe." The man did not say, as he might have done: What's she doing here, then, poking about with you? He had worries of his own. No wish to stir aggravation.

They moved on, passing within a few yards of where the crushing team worked. When they reached the gap in the fence the inspector managed to poke his head through. In the soft, crumbled earth left when three feet of towpath slid into the canal was the clear mark where a sole slithered.

Not much doubt about it—this is where Collie went in. No doubt at all that he was in the yard. Presumably, after dark.

Alone? Or was Arnold with him? Hmm.

He straightened, resettling the crutches under his armpits. "Right," he said. "Let's get back." And as the girl walked ahead, buttocks wagging as God decreed the nubile buttock must, he was visited by a sudden, intense flash from the past that set his traumatized libido up with a quite unexpected jump.

He saw a black stripper, in a club where he once sat disguised as an out-of-town lecher, waiting for the city police, who had borrowed him for the job, to burst in and bust all present. His part: to stay at the bar, making sure the barman had no chance to vanish all the liquor. Press of a button will do it, in well-organized clip joints.

She was very beautiful, the black girl, and very haughty. He saw again the high, pear-shaped breasts, the curve of belly, the triangle of black, crisp hair when she removed her G-string. He saw the glorious back, moving muscle highlighted under the black skin, buttocks mobile as those of the girl ahead. He saw the contempt in her fine-boned face and defensively arrogant eyes as she looked out over the heads of a chortling, obscenity-calling audience seeking lusty relief from the tedium of their lives and their wives, while she did unspeakable things with a banana. He saw all this and the girl crossing the oily wasteland ahead; and he felt, with something like shock, the stirring of an anatomical portion which, nowadays, never stirred.

Bloody hell, he thought: I wouldn't mind. I wouldn't mind at all. He spoke to the manager.

"Anything missing?"

"No," the manager said. "I told your other fellow—your Inspector Hocking." Very uneasy, he was. Well, he'd a few good things going here. So more than ever he stretched his salesman's smile. He'd been a good salesman. Wasn't a bad manager.

"Uh-huh." The inspector crutched on, unobtrusively flexing to ease the tightened trousers and thinking: What I'd like is to go through all your books, your stock—the lot. You're bent, lad.

The man Sam was down from his crane cab now, standing with the boy Albert, surveying the unstripped car, scratching his greasy head, and saying, "What stupid bastard put that there, then? That'll be that Dave and bloody Cecil." Dave and Cecil were two lads who stripped condemned cars down.

"What'll we do with it?" Albert asked.

"What do you bleeding think? If it starts, drive it

over by the fence, ask Mr. Ackers what he wants done with it."

Ten yards away, Mr. Ackers was passing with a gorilla in a black hat, on crutches. A wog bird walked ahead. Albert made a movement. Sam said, "Not now, stupid. Wait till he's free."

So Inspector Rosher passed within that little distance more twinkle than the boggled eye can absorb without dark glasses, and more kudos than will press a copper's cup down and run it over.

The Hagger party, except for the man himself, was quite surprised to find the Arnold Gutte party waiting in the rose garden of Bishop Adam Park. The very obvious nervous twitching of the small-town men caused Georgie to ask last night, on the way back to the city, "Whadda we do if dey scarper? Did one of us oughta stay to watch 'em?"

"What for?" his leader said. "They're not much good to us, are they? All we want from them is these herberts. And they can't find them."

"We can't find 'em on our tod, though, can we?" said Georgie. "I mean, we doan even know wod dey looks like."

"They won't scarper," Hagger said. "Not yet. They'll want a fair crack at the tickle." More, much more than they'd ever seen before, or ever would again. Hagger knew greed. Who better? He lived by it and with it.

"Yeah, but wod abaht dis copper, dis Roger dey was talkin' abaht?"

"What about him? He can't touch us for anything at all. If he whips in these little geezers—they don't even know our names, do they? First sign of trouble, we're gone."

"He cood pull us on suss." Suss equals suspicion.

"Got to catch us, hasn't he? Christ, Georgie, time to jack it in we get nobbled by a turnip basher on crutches."

So now they came into the rose garden and there were Arnold and Co., waiting by a Dorothy Perkins. Hagger wasted no time. "Good morning. Rung the hospital?"

"He's still in Intensive Care," said Arnold.

"Right. And no luck with your two herberts?"

"No."

"Uh-huh. All right. If Vennor isn't available by this afternoon, we have to get to him."

"How?"

Georgie put a word in. "We got our meffods."

"What about Rosher?" Ratface asked.

"We'll take care of him, if we have to." There was a grim look to Hagger as he said it. Did nothing to settle the nerves of Arnold and Ratface and Plonker. Nor did it help when he added, "What do the porters wear in this hospital? Or the maintenance men."

14

As soon as the funny-looking geezer like a bloody great monkey had inserted himself, his fat leg, and his crutches into a Mini and been driven off by the spade chick, leaving the manager standing in full view through the open yard gate cracking his knuckles, the man Sam said to the boy Albert, "All right—go and button him now."

So the boy Albert approached and said, " 'Scuse me, Mr. Ackers—there's a car with the heap, not stripped down."

"What's that, what's that?" said Mr. Ackers. "What's that?"

"Morris 1300. Not stripped."

"Who put it there?"

"I dunno. Not me," the boy Albert said, believing, as do all boys—and they are perfectly right—that the can comes ultimately to rest on the lowliest available shoulder.

"Get it stripped, then. Does it drive?"

"Yeah. We just drove it over by the fence." Sam did, the bastard. Never lets me have a go.

"Take it round to Dave and Cecil. No—hang on—where is it?" A drivable 1300, not stripped down. Always a proposition, the 1300.

The boy Albert moved with him toward the car.

Approaching it, the manager said, "All right—you can get back to work," and away the lad went.

As soon as the bonnet came up, the man thought: That's a bloody good engine. Doesn't belong in a 1300. He tried the steering. Nice and tight, no play. Not all sloppy, as a respectable car condemned has a right to be.

It's been rigged, he thought. That's a Renault engine. Very fast. Where'd it come from? And his mind, a thief leaping upon a thief, said: Bent. Somebody stashed it.

So who?

He walked away, thinking along several lines at once and saying as he passed the workers, "All right, Sam—leave it with me."

This ensured that the car would be left unmolested. He went into his office, sat at his desk, and continued to think. That engine—*exactly* what they wanted, him and Syd. They had this Renault, one of the expensive ones; bought in very cheap with a clapped engine and various corrosion areas needing considerable tarting; but promising high profit nicely doctored—especially with such a power unit. And as run-of-the-mill business, Syd had a 1300, a clear profit if it went back on the road with the steering assembly and better knick-knacks from this one; which had good wheels and tires and trims and exhaust and so on, and was in fair condition throughout, so far as he could see.

He should—of course he should, since there was no record of it in his books—report it to the police. But that would bring the bastards nosing around again. And this he did not need.

He had good things going. Private things that only he knew about—cars bought in cheap, listed as dear, and the difference pocketed. Mileages shown high in the book, to justify a low take-in price; turned back on the model way below the actual reading, to command a high selling figure; and again, into the trousers with the difference. A little petrol fiddle—a generally profitable setup; kept, ironically, from Elton Vennor, who was, Mr. Ackers believed, a bit of a mug and honest. Just as Mr. Vennor believed he was.

No: he did not want the police coming too close. Following on the geezer in the canal, they'd wonder exactly what he was wondering: was there a connection? That would have them sniffing much more closely than they would if it were merely a car reported as here without explanation.

He didn't want 'em here. He just didn't want 'em here, that's all.

On the other hand: he did want that Renault engine. So would Syd, if he saw it. Syd was his partner in a further small enterprise that few people knew about. A banger-tarting business. He had the bangers, forever streaming in and out of here. Syd had the skill, and the facilities. And Syd had a Renault all primed, lacking only a really good power unit to fetch maybe £2,000, tarted up and resprayed. He also had a condemned 1300. Give that new steering, a crisp box, good exhaust, and the rest—another five hundred, easy. Split it down the middle: £1,250 to him. More, because he'd reclaim from Syd half the figure he'd say he bought the car in for. All tax free.

Syd would know at once, of course, that the car had been rigged. But Syd wouldn't care a bugger, with that sort of profit in it. They'd handled a few suspected hots, in their time.

One snag: suppose it belonged to a gang, the feller who drowned only one of them? What if they came looking for it?

Well—he didn't know anything about it, did he? Most likely with one of them drowned they'd write it off. Presumably they had already, or why put it with the scrap? He'd say it must have gone through the crusher.

Thing to do: get it over to Syd's place. Get it looted, and the carcass returned for crushing. Knock it about a bit, those stupid bastards out there would never recognize it.

He got up and went to the office door. Looked around. Nobody about. He'd just have a word with Syd on the blower, regarding immediate collection. He could arrive during tea break.

When he finished his call he stepped out into the scrapyard and said, "Sam—that jalopy. Run it up on the concrete when you've got a minute. It must have bypassed Dave and Cecil."

"Yeah. Right," called Sam, from the cab of his crane.

Mr. Ackers walked back toward his office. That was it—the jalopy vanished, they'd assume Dave and Cecil collected it. Useful, the boss being in the hospital, it gave him a free hand. He might have hesitated on this one, if the bastard had been around. Crossing the concrete area, he glanced at Collie's car. The one that had stood with it was gone into the workshops, the owner having telephoned instructions. Presumably somebody would ring soon about this one, to say what he wanted done to it.

If Vennor snuffed—and they reckoned he might, Intensive Care and all—presumably his missus'd take over. Didn't know a thing about the business, did she? It'd all be up to him.

Ho ho. The good days could be coming. There was a lot he could do that he couldn't do now. Like two sets of books.

What's more: he'd often thought he'd like a bash at Mrs. Vennor. Big tits, randy legs. But you don't foul your own nest.

A hungry widow, though ... You never knew—he might even marry into Managing Director.

Ho ho. Ho ho. Three businesses she'd have, if hubby snuffed it.

Oh no. He didn't want the Old Bill sniffing, at a time like this. Apart from the profit in it: get that jalopy out of here.

Detective Inspector Rosher, when he alighted at the hospital, settled onto his crutches and swung his body up the steps. Getting quite nimble at it, by now. Nurse Holness came beside him. She led him past the reception desk and into the gleaming passage that leads, if you persevere, to a ward and to various departments dedicated to the relief of unsavory malfunctions, and terminates in the Intensive Care Unit. As life itself often does.

They did not go that far. In one of the waiting rooms en route sat people who were here to have their heads pored over. Several wore bandages. Some wore crew cuts, growing since the skull was shaved. All glanced up glumly when the girl came in with the man on crutches. One looked hard at the black hat worn low upon the brow, as if suspecting that it hid an ice pick, stuck in the top of the head. Or a hand of bananas.

The girl said, "Stay here a minute," and she went on to exit through a door beyond the benches. It gave momentary view, when she opened it, of sterilized things and a rackful of bottles. Inspector Rosher disconcerted with hard little eyes the man who was staring at his hat. The man smiled weakly. "I fell out of my cradle," he said.

"What?" barked Rosher. All the people looked at him again.

"Window cleaning. I was window cleaning. Fourth floor."

"Lucky you wasn't killed," said a lady with a felt hat over her crew cut.

"Thought I was, at first," the man said, "but I bounced off a milk float. Nine weeks flat on my back with it. Well, ten if you count the last."

Why wouldn't I? Rosher thought; but all he said was,

"Hrrmph." He then pulled out his great gray sheet of handkerchief while they all sat there unguarded, and blew such a blast as set them quivering upright on the benches when they came down. It couldn't have done their poor heads any good. Beyond the door, the nurse who was speaking to the West Indian nurse started and said, "Christ! What's that?"

"It's all right," soothed Nurse Holness. "It's only Mr. Rosher."

"What does he do it with?"

"His nose. He blows it."

"He ought to have that looked at, while he's here. He's got time, because as I say, Mr. Harnett's gone out. Emergency."

"When will he be back?"

"Don't know, do I? It's jammed up a bit, old Mrs. Grommand's been waiting since half-past nine. Can't jump your case in now, you should have brought him earlier. Look—give us a ring after lunch. We may be able to fit him in this afternoon."

"Yes—thanks," said Nurse Holness. "I'll do that." She turned away, opened the door, and reappeared to the people in the waiting room. "Come back after lunch," she told Rosher.

"Hnnnn," he said.

"Well, I told you we should come straight here," she retorted, almost defensively. When his brows came down and he made that noise through his nose it had this effect on people. Even people like herself, who had no reason to feel guilty. Heck, she was doing him a favor. "You did it yourself." She moved to the door and held it open while he heaved himself through. The man who spent all those weeks on his back said when the door was shut, "Funny-looking feller. Puts me in mind of a circus."

The lady with the crew cut simpered. "Wouldn't want to meet him on a dark night," she said. "Specially if he had to blow his nose." And she adjusted her felt hat, complacently accepting the nods and smiles of the assembled company as merited tribute to her wit. For a few golden seconds it was quite gay in here, using the word in its better sense. Old Mrs. Grommand actively cackled; thinking: What I like about hospitals, you do get a bit of company. Which you don't sitting in front of the telly. Maybe, she told herself, it was a good thing she fell on her head trying to adjust the vertical hold, even though she'd been falling over, one way and another, ever since.

When they were in her small car, Rosher said to Nurse Holness, "What do we do now, then?"

"Well," she said, rather nonplussed. "I suppose I'd better run you home." He could get a taxi, or something, to bring him back later.

"Hmm." He shot his little eyes sideways at her. "Er—you busy? I mean—what are you doing after this?"

"Nothing, really. Not till this evening. Mum's gone to stay with Uncle Ignatius." The house is empty. And cold. Filled with Benjie and sorrow. I might try a cinema.

"Ah. Mm. I've got beefburgers. In the fridge. Plenty of crinkle chips." Baked beans—tins of spaghetti—marmalade. Need some bread, that's all. "I could—er—cook 'em up." Had he known of Nefertiti, he would have observed that this girl had the same slim and glorious neck and was very like her in profile. He knew she was beautiful; he knew he didn't want her to go. His house, too, was empty, and chilled with its own emptiness. Mind you, that was better than having it full of fat wife.

She turned to look at him; thinking, with sudden insight: he's lonely. He doesn't want to be left on his own. And she smiled. "I'm anybody's," she said, "for a beefburger."

"Ah," he said. "I mean—that's what I've got in. I

could—we could stop on the way, get a couple of steaks—"

"And I bet you'd cook 'em twenty minutes each side in that dirty old frying pan. You get a couple of steaks, I'll do the cooking."

So this is exactly what she did. And more.

Arnold Gutte, too, at about this time was doing a little shopping. At a secondhand-and-surplus store in a street called, appropriately, Cheap Row, he was buying three sets of used overalls. Boiler suits, washed and in what the store described as serviceable condition, but with stains on. While Georgie stood watch outside to ensure that he did as he'd been told, he also bought a metal toolbox. Nothing in it, just the box.

This morning, Jack Hagger had made him ring the hospital again; and the hospital said there was some improvement in Mr. Vennor's condition. That he was, in fact, conscious. Hagger had said, "All right. If he's conscious he can talk. So we have to get to him. Where did you say this boiler-suit shop is?"

"Cheap Row," he'd said. "But—er—just because he's conscious don't mean he can talk . . ." He was still in Intensive Care.

"Just leave the planning to me, sonny," the cold-eyed Hagger said. "Just leave it to me."

"Yes, but—" Arnold began; Georgie interrupted.

"You 'eard wot de guv'nor sedd."

There is no standing against the combined weight of three big men from London who go armed with Lugers, every day. Not if you are small-time, and small-town; and with these truths forced brutally before your eyes, wishing to Christ you were in Stoke Poges. Or Bombay, or Caracas. Anyplace. But not here. How in Christ did you ever get mixed up in it, you ask yourself, thinking you were a leader and all? You must have been bloody mad.

He came out from the store with a bundle under his arm, holding the toolbox in his free hand. Georgie, standing where he was just out of sight from inside the shop, said, "Goddem? Good. Come on, den," and led the way back to where Arnold's car stood, tucked around a corner out of sight. Five minutes later they rejoined the main party, just out of town in a lay-by. Hagger inspected the goods briefly and said, "Uh-huh. They'll do. Now: we go to lunch. Give it an hour or two, then you can ring again. Check that they haven't moved him. Maybe he'll be chattering like a myna bird by then. You must know a pub or something, an out-of-the-way restaurant. We'll go there. But not all together—we'll go in pairs. And we don't know each other. When I get up to go, you give it a couple of minutes, Mr. Brown. You do the same, Mr. Green, after Mr. Brown."

Very sensible. Three big men and three jittery ones, all entering together to dominate the available space, attract considerable attention. Also: the three jittery men are not likely to gather themselves to revolt or a sudden swift scarper between the tables if you keep them separated. Divide and conquer.

Rosher bought two very good steaks, the girl saw to that. She also made him buy mushrooms and various exotics which he never would have bought for himself, partly because he would never have thought of it or known what to do with them if he had, and partly because they come a damn sight dearer than cabbage. Today, once he had swallowed hard and grunted several times, he did not grudge the expense. She had, after all, saved him paying for taxis.

He actually enjoyed the shopping. It moved him, somehow, to watch her slim hands reaching out to select the best and to receive the packages, the fine absorption with which she concentrated; and the shape of buttocks under her jeans, high breasts under her sweater, kept his reawakened libido on the trot. The bottle of Spanish wine was his own idea. Sod the expense, it's a poor heart that never rejoices. And the kid had lost a brother, she needed cheering up a bit.

A measure of her effect upon him lies in the very fact of his considering her pain at all. Nobody ever called him a sensitive man. Nobody ever called him less than self-centered; and the most simpatico of policemen, during a lifetime of work in a field where violent and ugly death is the daily norm, grows a protective skin as armor against personal involvement with grief, or goes mad. He had survived without going mad.

She could cook, no doubt about that. She served a lunch the like of which had not come his way since the day of his fat wife or, more recently, the brothel madam who lived in briefly; and whom she might well, given a little time, nudge out of his dreams. But before she used them she scoured all the pans and the cooker. "I wonder you haven't poisoned yourself," she said. "Ought to be able to wash a pot, great big man like you." And after lunch, when he had wiped to her washing up, "Look—I can't stand this muddle. You better sit down—I'm going to clean up a bit."

Well, he didn't mind. He huffed and gruffed a little; but the truth is, her tough-minded scolding—nurses learn to be tough-minded, and to abhor squalid disorder—set up a chuckle in his belly. And, of course, anybody who chose to restore seemliness to his domestic environment was more than welcome to try.

So he sat well fed and contented, and felt his long-supine appendage swell to the changing curves of her body as she stretched up with a duster, bent to dustpan and brush, whirred his Hoover around; seeing in his mental eye that black stripper, transferring naked-nesses. Not with deliberate stoking of furtive lust, but because the man who does not see, by God's grace, a desirable woman naked when they are private in his house is past redemption and bound for the pit.

I wonder, he said to himself, what she'd do if I made a pass? She must like me. Mustn't she? Or she wouldn't have come, she wouldn't be here.

But: sod it. Don't be a twat—you've had trouble enough from women. Besides, she must be—what?— thirty years younger than you. Nearer forty.Well— thirty-five.

Mind you, some of 'em go for older men.

Wonder if she'll notice if I ease my trousers?

Besides: what can you do, on bloody crutches?

In the middle of vacuuming she broke off, and without so much as a by-your-leave picked up his telephone. Perhaps it is the transvestite element that makes of tight jeans such a potent garment when worn by woman. In place of the crotch bulge proper to man is one sweet curve between the long, denim-divided thighs. He enjoyed her as she stood upright and breasted, speaking into the phone. When she put it down, she said, "Three o'clock. You can go straight in. Just gives me time to finish off here. You ought to arrange to have a woman every day."

The obvious arch rejoinder flicked through his mind. Once he would have uttered it, asking if she'd like to volunteer. But now—no. She might giggle, and simper, and go all girlish as she protested—hypocritically, in the normal feminine manner?—that she hadn't meant that.

No. It would all spoil. He'd sooner not know, if she was giving him the crude come-on line. It would destroy a sort of frank and forthright delicacy that he was prizing in her. And besides: in spite of the up-and-at-'em motion down where it counts, he was not at all sure that after all this time, all those calamities foisted upon him by the ravening appendage, he could actually perform. No greater embarrassment than to find that he could not.

At a quarter to three they left his relatively spick-and-span house—that sort of mess cannot be properly cleaned up in an hour, and she never even looked upstairs—and shut themselves back into her little car to set off again for the hospital. Arrived there at five to three, and he was closeted with Mr. Harnett by a quarter past.

They lingered over their separate lunches until half past two, Hagger and Arnold here, at a table in the pub window; George and Ratface over there, Charles and Joe "Plonker" Milgrave farther along the bar. The three local men had agreed that the Black Bull in the town center would suit better than any of the restaurants. It has a buffet bar that virtually is a restaurant, very popular with tourists and local businessmen who bring strangers in, visiting executives to be hosted to the famous Black Bull steak pie, or the equally meritorious beef casserole with dumplings. Best food in town, and a nice change from restaurants.

It was not appreciated today by the three local men. They left most of it on the plates. And by Hagger's edict, there was no lavish alcohol intake to give them Dutch courage. All they were allowed was a pint each, and the London men saw they stuck at that. Hagger himself seemed to enjoy the meal, though. He said as he rose to leave, "Ah. Good pie, very good. Let's go, then."

He drained his glass and led the way. Arnold followed him to where the big smart car stood, just across the road in the town square. General parking ground, except on market day. At the end of two minutes, Georgie appeared with Ratface Rorke. Charles and Plonker would be gathering themselves inside. Hagger said, "Right. The phone box over there. Make the call. We'll change in the car."

Arnold's already strained nerves jumped. "We?"

"You're coming in with us, boyo. He knows you better than he does me. Got the change? I'll be waiting outside." Better, in case of brouhaha following, for all calls inquiring after Vennor to have been made in one unremarkable local voice than to introduce a London accent.

This last straw loaded onto his back broke Arnold. Ever since he saw the Lugers he had been stuck nastily between cupidity and the sure knowledge that these men were highly dangerous—to him and his associates especially, because whatever they chose to do, he had no way to prevent it. They were in a different league; and they'd certainly scarper when it was all done, particularly if it went bad. Leaving him and his still here. Unable to scarper, because to do so with Rosher peering would be fatal.

They were frightening. They'd more or less said they'd blow Rosher away. That'd be nice. Kill a copper and you're right in the heap.

And more than this: he and Ratface and Plonker: they didn't know the geezers' names—not Smith and Brown and Green, for sure—but they knew what they looked like. Picked up, they could supply detailed descriptions.

So: picked up they might be. Out of a river or something, a neat little hole behind the ear. Because there was very, very big tickle involved. Men have killed often and often for much less; especially to avoid paying cuts and to obtain silence, all at one stroke.

And now: he was to be coerced into the visit to Vennor; and what did they intend to do to that man when they got there? Talk to him, they said. How? It could kill him. Couldn't it?

That'd be manslaughter, surely. Or would it? Anyway—it could kill him. Just having them shoving at him.

Whatever happened, in any direction, meant terrible trouble for Arnold. Since Mr. Smith revealed his plan, he had been given no chance to confer with his mates. He'd been ordered to Mr. Smith's car, while Mr. Brown and Mr. Green both traveled in his car with

Ratface and Plonker. They were being kept apart, deliberately. And that made his flesh crawl.

He walked now to the handy phone booth, the terrible man beside him, with his mind churning toward panic. Why, oh why hadn't he done as Collie must have done: scarpered clean out of it?

Because he never had the chance, that's why. He'd been stuck, thinking they were coppers. "Right," said the man at his side as they reached the booth. "Don't be too long. All we need to know is: is he talking?"

Panic, of course, is the enemy of clear thinking. There were still things that Arnold could have done to circumvent that mission. Because Hagger did not enter the booth with him, to hear the conversation. Put that down, if you wish, as a flaw in his planning; due, perhaps to overconfidence in himself, his henchmen, and the power in the Lugers, plus contempt for these little men from a minor league.

Remember, though, that it takes time to work out a truly copper-bottomed plan. Time Hagger did not have, he was doing the best he could almost by ear; and having the normal criminal obsession with personal anonymity in time of action, he'd reasoned that one little man in a box is hardly there at all; but two men crushed into that box become notable.

So Arnold could have made no call at all. He could have faked, and emerged to say that Vennor was dead, or dying, or relapsed, or moved to somewhere inaccessible. He could have said the police were with him.

Or could he? What if Hagger rang forthwith, to check? Come to think of it, with this kind of twinkle at stake, he almost certainly would.

Hmm. Perhaps Arnold, churning with panic, did the right thing after all, from his own point of view. He fumbled money into the slot with shaking fingers, and learned that Vennor was still under intensive care but marginally better; and as he said thank you, he thought: Christ—what if it kills him? We'll be—I'll be—done for—murder? Manslaughter? Christ knows what. Life. I might get fucking life.

Grass. Grass—it's the only thing. Rosher... The Old Bill. The beak'll go easy if I grass—a year—two years—for involvement in armed robbery—nobody got hurt. Tell 'em you've been lumbered with this—tell 'em he's got a gun on you.

He did not replace the phone. Very furtively, with his eyes screwed sideways to Hagger waiting outside, he hunched a shoulder to conceal the finger with which he broke the connection and immediately dialed 999. That took some doing, his hand was shaking so. Answer was immediate. He said, "Police!" Click, and they were there.

"Listen," he babbled. "They're going to raid—the hospital—now—"

"Hospital?" the lady policeman on the station switchboard said. "Who—"

"Guns," Arnold said in that babbly whisper. "They've got guns—"

"One moment—"

"Guns—guns—"

Hagger moved a pace, reached out for the handle of the door.

"May I have your name, sir, please?" the girl said.

The door was opening. Hagger was snapping, "What's taking so long?" Impatience is natural to a leader, at a time like this. The seconds hang fire when you are keyed for action.

"Just coming," said Arnold, and left the girl flat. Hung up quick, in case her squawking voice carried, and gave him away. He could feel the iced sweat running down his back. His face felt wet, cold and clammily stiff. He said, emerging from the booth, "He's— he's still there."

"Conscious?"

"Yes."

"Right. Let's get moving."

Arnold could not see the equally hapless Ratface and Plonker, but he knew where they were. They'd been ushered into his car, and were sitting there with Messrs. Brown and Green. His quivering buttocks met genuine leather upholstery as his own guardian slid in behind the wheel. In the rearview mirror, as the car moved out and paused before taking the road, he saw his car following. The man beside him spoke.

"You know the town. Think of a quiet corner, on the way. We'll change into the overalls there."

15

There were two patients only waiting for the attention of Mr. Harnett when Nurse Holness held the door open so that Detective Inspector Rosher could lever himself again into the waiting room. Those here this morning were gone, these were quite different. No bandages, even, and the hair well grown, if it was ever shaven. Nurse Holness said, "Ah. Good. He won't be long. Sit here, and I'll come back for you." Wine with lunch brings afternoon thirst. She was dying for a cup of tea.

A nurse in her own hospital stands on ground entitling her to a certain bossiness. Rosher eased himself down onto one of the benches, well away from the other two casualties. She left him there with his eyes irritable under the black hat. This wasn't going straight in. Still, he supposed she'd done her best. Just so long as he didn't have to sit here all afternoon.

She went back along the corridor, passing the door to the Upshawe Ward, named for Upshawe of Upshawe's Patent Corn Cure; who when he died of something horrible left a tittle of his considerable fortune (business boomed when people took to wearing plastic shoes) to its endowment. There would be tea in the nurses' room, there always was.

Yes. There was. She poured a cup and sat in one of

the decent little chairs, bequest of Miss Ruckinstone. Parkinson's disease, 1958. As she sipped, the sister from her own ward came in, and said, "Oh—hallo, Jenny. Having tea?" Off duty, her nurses redonned their informal names.

"Just a cup, Sister. I was passing by."

"Uh-huh. I think I'll have one, while I'm here." Sister poured. It was what she came for. Catch her off the job, she was much less starched. "Er—I expect they've told you—we've got the boy who—er—was responsible for your brother. Downstairs. Burns."

"*We've* got him? They said he was at the police station, how'd he get burns?"

"Not that one—the other one. The one they were looking for, apparently. Seems he pulled somebody out of a blazing car. Stock car racing."

"Ah." Nobody had told her. But then, she'd been out of touch since she came off duty, early this morning. Actually, Mike's identity was known long before that. Since yesterday evening, when talk with various drivers told the promoter he had given the wrong name. He rang the police, not because he knew that Mike was wanted, but because he needed to keep the record straight. Stock car racing is a dodgy business, you have to keep in with the police.

"Nobody's all bad, you see." Sister was a committed Christian, and so honor-bound to advance charity, except to those who left bits of fluff under the bed or dust on a lampshade. "They say he was quite the hero. He's in Upshawe Ward."

"Ah." Right opposite where she left Rosher, her visit to and ferrying about of whom she did not mention. It was, as she'd said, unethical.

Sister drank quickly, as is the way with energetic and busy people. She then bustled out, with a cheery word. Nurse Holness finished her tea and followed, after a trip to the lavatory. Strange, the things Fate chooses to set up a situation. It would all have been different, but for Nurse Holness's bladder. Taken in conjunction, of course, with the brave act that landed Mike Gibbins in Upshawe Ward, and Inspector Rosher's presence here. A series of seemingly unrelated happenings all coalescing, the final timing manipulated by sending a girl to a lavatory. And a man. But that came later.

Hagger's party stopped briefly in a quiet place on the way, while Hagger and Arnold, and Georgie in the other car, wriggled into the overalls. When they arrived in the hospital car park, Charles, in his suit, entered the building first, leaving Georgie to guard Ratface and Plonker—almost openly treated as prisoners now, as was Arnold in Hagger's car.

No need for Hagger to tell his men what to do, the plan was made. Besides, they'd done similar things before. Charles was away for a few minutes only. When he emerged he came to Hagger, speaking through the open window.

"Turn right through the reception hall. There's a sign."

"Uh-huh," said Jack Hagger. Charles went back to Arnold's car. After a look around—people might wonder, seeing two overalled men climb out of such a very decent car—Hagger said to Arnold as he opened the door, "This is it, then, sonny. We'll show you how the big boys do it. No need to shit yourself, just get out and act normally. You can carry the toolbox." Still nothing in that box. Window dressing only. What actors call a hand prop.

Charles was getting into the other car by now, settling behind the wheel while boiler-suited Georgie came out. The gentleman's gentleman would stay, to look after the little men and to take off in the wake of the active participants when they came back and drove away in Hagger's car. Better a cool hand behind the wheel than entrust it to a little feller so scared he runs straight into the gatepost before he even hits the road.

With Arnold in the middle, then, carrying the metal box, the three overalled men walked up the steps, through the doors, and into the reception hall, where, as Charles had promised, was a sign.

They turned right and moved along the corridor, passing within a few feet of not only Detective Inspector Rosher, but, on the other side, the lad who could have told them where he stashed the car, and exactly what car to look for. Lying there for all to see, he was, or would have been had they not closed the curtains around him: the tearaway they spent an entire evening seeking. A lady policeman sitting by his bed; but what is a lady policeman, to men like these?

Nobody took any notice as they walked on toward the Intensive Care Unit. Men in boiler suits are a common sight in hospitals, working there or visiting mates mangled in pursuit of the daily bread. They sit and talk of football, or pigeon racing, or the likely amount of industrial compensation to be screwed out of the boss.

It must be understood that when Fate gathers all these strings together at the climax, things happen simultaneously much quicker than they can be written down. Thus the growing press on Inspector Rosher's bladder—he'd been feeling pressure for some time—grew to urgency even as the men went by; which was when Nurse Holness, her own urgency jettisoned but sitting there still while she touched up her face, put lipstick and compact back into her shoulder-strap handbag and stood up to adjust her dress before leaving; which she did as Hagger, faced with three doors at the end of the corridor, opened one and peered in. Somebody who looked dead lay there. It wasn't Vennor, but it could have been somebody's grandma. A nurse came out from one of the other doors, stopped in her tracks, and said indignantly, "What do you think you're doing?"

"Where's Mr. Vennor?" Hagger said.

"Mr. Vennor cannot be visi—"

"Don't fuck me about, lady," said Gentleman Jack Hagger. "Where's Vennor?"

"You can't—" she began, and then her eyes widened. Because he grabbed her, clapped a hand over her mouth. "Vennor," he snarled, "or I'll break your bloody back." A good deal of his nice accent had left him.

Those wide eyes suddenly frightened—she was a white girl, so they were a beautiful cornflower blue— she managed to indicate the third door. She really need not have bothered. Georgie had shoved Arnold forward. His gun was in his hand now, and he used it to indicate that Arnold should open the door. Arnold did.

"You scream, darling," Hagger told his nurse, "and you get a bullet in the spine. Move." He shoved her ahead, into the room. Georgie slipped in with him, shepherding Arnold, who was by now too shattered to do anything about anything. During a bent lifetime he had run himself into dangers, he had carried guns, but never without yea or nay over his own participation, never with men so frighteningly reckless as this.

The ward was not very big, about twice the size of a decent living room; but it contained four beds, two of them occupied, a great deal of electronic equipment, and a plump nurse. Intensive care units are normally built open-plan, to facilitate watch over all of the people all of the time. In separate cubicles they could snuff, and you'd not know it until you peeked in.

The nurse here, plump and comfy-looking, stretched her eyes as they came in, her mouth a little round rosebud. In one of the beds lay Vennor, wired to a cardiac monitor and with an oxygen mask over his face. Arnold knew him at once. His eyes were open and he was looking this way.

Hagger did not, never having met the man eyeball to eyeball. All their dealing had been by go-between—that poor little jeweler's manager, gone now on a holiday abroad with his unaware wife, to be out of the way of any post-robbery heat. So the gang man said to the nurse, "Vennor. Which is Vennor?" Either of the beds could have been containing him. Both incumbents were male.

Georgie shut the door. The plump nurse said, "What the—what—?"

Hagger's gun was out now. He snarled at her. "Vennor. Which is Vennor?" He poked the gun into the back of the girl he was holding and said before releasing her, "You make a sound, darling, I shoot your liver out."

The plump nurse showed no sign of starting into hysterical screaming, perhaps because she was too astonished, or perhaps because sudden screaming in an intensive care unit can nullify a lot of effort gone into keeping the cared-for alive. She glared at the big man, little mouth set and chin quivering. Hagger snapped at Arnold. "Which is Vennor?"

Arnold pointed. His erstwhile leader lay propped on pillows, eyes very dark and solemn, looking straight at him. The graph needle of his cardiac monitor flickered a jazzy line. Hagger crossed to him. The monitor attached to the bed next to his gave forth suddenly a high, continuous note. The poor sod attached had died. Excitement? Shock? The plump nurse moved. Hagger barked, "Stay there!"

But the nurse came on, she couldn't just let the man perish untimely. Up went Hagger's arm, to bring the heavy gun barrel crashing down on her skull. She dropped in a plump and crumpled heap. The second nurse's hands flew to her mouth and she made a little whimper. Hagger turned to the man in the bed. The live one. "Vennor," he said, "listen—the car—where's the car?"

Vennor made a noise, half raising himself from the

pillows: an inarticulate sound muffled by the oxygen mask. Hagger reached, to tear it away.

And now Arnold moved, crying out of risen panic, "No—no—you'll kill him—" He started forward.

Hagger's gun swung again: backhand, almost horizontal. It smashed into Arnold's mouth. He staggered back, bumping into the nurse, who automatically clutched him to avoid her own falling. He leaned against her, dazed, spitting front teeth and blood from his mashed lips. Hagger turned again to the bed.

"Vennor—Vennor—listen—"

Vennor reached out his hand, straining to raise himself. And all the time his wife slumbered in that little room next door, worn out with watching over him. "Gler-ugh," he said. "I've . . . I've . . ." His eyes wobbled as he fell back. The line on his monitor screen straightened abruptly, and the machine joined the other in a thin, continuous bleep.

It had all gone wrong. Hagger and Georgie knew it; had even, in a sense, been prepared for it, as class professionals always are. What they had not reckoned on was barred windows. They'd thought to leave by the windows.

But no matter, it was not far along that corridor. Abort the whole enterprise now. The right word from Vennor, and they'd have made, according to plan, one fast swoop and away before pursuit could sort itself out. Who would know where they'd gone, once they left here? They'd take the yokel lads with them, vanish them if need be in London.

The word had not come. The shrill machines were crying urgent summons. No option but to abort. Professionals do not need to confer. Hagger addressed the nurse and Arnold.

"You walk ahead. Hold your handkerchief over that mouth. And remember: there are two guns on you."

No way of knowing if those keening machines were linked up elsewhere. Some brave twat of a doctor might be rushing this way even now. A gun in the back of a nurse is good insurance.

They came out from the room, closing the door to minimize the bleeping. Nobody about, except a cripple on crutches, moving along with his back toward them, wearing a black hat.

A nurse passing through had told Inspector Rosher of a lavatory just along the corridor. He had propelled himself there as fast as his crutches would trot, passing on the way the entrance of Upshawe Ward. It was a few yards farther along the passage than his waiting room, on the opposite side; and inside the ward was Nurse Holness.

She had deflected, on her way back to collect Rosher. She must see this lad. She must see what sort of youth comes upon a quiet boy on a quiet night and kills him, just like that.

Upshawe is a small ward. Mike Gibbins lay in a bed up in the far corner. She knew it would be the one, because the curtains were drawn around it. In her ward, certainly, a patient guarded on a police charge would be in the bed with curtains drawn. In a private room, had one been available; but in hospitals these days this is rarely possible. She pushed through the curtains. A youngish woman in plain clothes sat by the bed. Her name, if it matters, was Sergeant Mossy. Mavis Mossy. She said, "What do you want?"

"It's all right," said Nurse Holness. "I'm a nurse." So this was him, lying small and vulnerable on his back, thickly bandaged arms above the bedclothes. No eyebrows, they had been singed off. It gave him a very young, almost babyish look. His eyes, staring at her, were clear, child-blue.

"Ah," said Sergeant Mossy. "You're not in uniform."

The girl addressed the patient. "Why did you do it? Why did you kill my brother?"

He gazed at her with no apparent emotion. If the

confrontation disturbed him, he was not letting it show. The sergeant said, "Your brother?"

"He murdered my brother."

"Oh." The woman hesitated. "Er—I'm afraid—"

"It's all right," said Nurse Holness. "I—just wanted to see what sort of . . ." She turned to go; turned back and spoke again to the boy. "Tell me one thing. Would you have killed him if he hadn't been black?"

"Piss off," said Mike, and turned his head away.

Inspector Rosher came from the lavatory—it appeared to have been designed for women, but in times of great need who stops to dwell on gender?—and began the ten-yard trek back to his waiting room. Now that he could think again of things other than his fundamental distress, he wondered as he went if he might buy more steaks, more wine. Or a chicken, or something; and if she would come back, and cook it, and eat it with him. He had some candles somewhere. She would look good, eating with him by candlelight. She'd said something about being busy this evening, but—well—she seemed to like her lunch. . . .

As he opened the waiting room door, which was not easy because of his crutches, he chanced to turn his head. Quite casually, just glancing along the corridor. Coming along it were two big geezers, a man holding a handkerchief to his mouth, and a rather pretty nurse.

Now, there is nothing so very unusual in an injury accompanied by a nurse walking along a hospital corridor. What made this pair outstanding was: the nurse looked frightened, and the casualty was Arnold Gutte. No doubt about it, in spite of the handkerchief and the boiler suit.

What was Arnold Gutte doing in a boiler suit, injured, and walking along here with a nurse and two big boiler-suited geezers behind? The inspector said, in quite a Blubbergut bark, "Arnold!"

So it was actually Rosher who triggered the ensuing

seconds of violent action. Well, he should not be blamed. He spoke to startle, and this is a legitimate policemanly ploy. A suspect startled is wrong-footed from the beginning.

You can say the ploy succeeded only too well. The outcome hinged upon a paradox. Your small-time bent feel toward the police hatred and fear; and this adds up, however they would deny it, to respect. Certain coppers who loom large in their life are peculiarly subject to it. In Arnold's life, Rosher loomed large, particularly since he appeared on crutches in a flash and a whiff of brimstone, to hint darkly.

The paradox lies here: in spite of lifelong enmity to law and order, when he needs it himself the bent runs automatically to the police; imbued, even as you and I, with the belief that there stands Father, stern but just, empowered and able to quell the circumstances threatening the child. A surprising thing about the small-time bent: they are infinitely childlike. Face facts—every child is bent.

Now pay attention, because what happened next happened so fast that if you don't you'll miss it. Events were more or less simultaneous. Arnold, if he did not see salvation, at least saw Father, suddenly here in another whiff of brimstone. He bleated, "Mr. Rosher—Mr. Rosher—" and began to run: toward the apelike figure huddled on the crutches. Hagger's hand left the pocket of his boiler suit and he fired that Luger just as Nurse Holness reached the door of Upshawe Ward, almost at his elbow.

The bullet hit Arnold in the shoulder as the captive nurse screamed shrilly, shot and scream together re-echoing from walls and ceiling and clacking floor of the naked corridor. Arnold's sobbing cry mingled as he fell, the bullet ricocheting from his shoulder blade to whang against a fire extinguisher mounted on the wall, and thence to Rosher's black hat. Good job he was wearing it, or that nasty piece of lead would have buried itself in his skull. Durable but not bulletproof.

The hat leaped. A new parting in his short-back-and-sides, Rosher fell sideways from the shock, crutches flying with a clatter as Hagger aimed again. At him, on the floor.

Whether he meant to murder, or merely to issue armed warning, is a debatable point never to be clarified. Because Nurse Holness swung her shoulder bag—by instinct, it must have been, she really had no time to think—by the strap, under and up. It hit Hagger's outstretched forearm. The elbow joint does not hold rigid against a surprise blow. Up came the gun and went off—was the finger tightening, to blow Rosher or/and Arnold away, or did it twitch as the result of the blow?—and shot Jack Hagger right through the eye; above and behind which is the brain.

Hagger fell, right at the feet of the screaming nurse; and now Georgie, gun out and in hand, started to run as panic took him. The noise alone was enough to terrify. Two steps he took and hurdled the sobbing Arnold; two more and he fell over a crutch, clattered from Rosher out into the corridor. The gun flew from his hand, and as he scrambled to get up, up, and away the inspector, shocked and dazed, nevertheless somehow managed to squirm and grab an ankle to fell him again.

Outside, P.C. Wally Wargrave and his oppo, P.C. Gordon Kenton, were entering the building from the car park. Unarmed; but they were cruising in the nearest patrol car when the call came from the station. There is only one gate in and out of the car park, and with commendable intelligence they left the car sideways across, to block it; at which Charles, in Arnold's car, seeing them half run across to the building, said, "Jesus Christ," and drew his gun. He didn't know what was going on, of course, because the noise did not carry that far.

Screaming told the policemen which way to go from

the reception hall, where all the startled faces pointed one way. In the corridor they found a white nurse screaming above what looked like a body; a black girl wide-eyed and open-mouthed with a shoulder bag swinging from her hand; a man lying down, clutching his shoulder and sobbing; and a snarling gorilla squatted with a pottery leg stuck out on the back of a face-down man who was losing blood. The gorilla—Christ, it was Blubbergut—had hands twined into the man's hair and was smashing his face into the highly polished hygienic parquet, again and again and again. The man was prone, not struggling.

P.C. Wargrave leaped forward, to wrench the berserk apeman off by main force. No mean task. "For Christ's sake," he said, "you'll kill the poor sod—you'll kill him." P.C. Kenton was picking up the gun.

An interval ensued before the next brief action. Put this down to Charles, sitting racked with indecision.

He should have taken off straight away. Forget mechanized transport—he could have gone over the fence, made for the railway station, hopped on a convenient bus. He could have told the yokels to make their own way out—they would, no doubt, have followed him over the fence, if no farther—and simply vanished. But things held him.

First: if Hagger and Georgie arrived back in London, they would not beam upon him if he'd scarpered. They might come out from that hospital any minute with those coppers at gunpoint, calling upon him to grab the ignition key and clear the car out of the gateway, so that they could all zoom off together.

Second: Charles really did have flair, as valet. He liked it; and men who like valeting and hairdressing and stewarding on ships are as often as not, however bulky, latently if not actively queer. Charles was not active; but he did have very deep attachment to, enormous admiration for, the powerfully potent, ut-

terly butch Jack Hagger. You could say—why not?—
that he loved him. We do not desert, unless we must,
the loved one in peril.

So he sat indecisive until chance had passed him by;
waiting for somebody to come out, wondering if he
should go in; deciding against it for fear of what these
two yokel herberts would do as soon as his back was
turned. And nobody came.

Why would they? When people get shot in a hospital—and how rare an event this is—you don't rush
them about outside. You whisk them into wards. Or
the morgue, should they qualify. This was being done,
while he sat gun in hand if only to keep the local lads in
order, and worked himself into a sweat. And this indecision cost him his chance.

Because things were not standing still in the outside
world. One after the other, two more police cars
had arrived, sirens screaming and roof lights aflash.
One was right outside the fence now, you could see it
through the open palings. Two uniformed men from
the other were out, and standing behind that car blocking the gateway. So bang went any chance of going
over the fence.

Then came the reason why the unarmed men had,
presumably, been told by radio to hold back, to stay at
the gate. A minibus, screeching like a banshee with
men aboard. Four of them, leaping out; and two held
rifles. Somebody at the station had taken Arnold's call
seriously. Though why, for Christ's sake, sober men
were asking themselves, raid a flipping hospital?
Drugs?

One of the riflemen hurried toward the building,
accompanied by a man in a suit who, no doubt, had a
pistol on him. The other man with a rifle stayed at the
gate, and the fourth climbed into that exit-blocking
car, to drive it aside.

And now Charles decided to go. Something was
gravely awry. Get out now, while the main gunning

force was away. Drive slow and easy to the gate; accelerate when the bastards wave you down. They can't shoot at you until you shoot at them.

All this time, he had not spoken to Plonker and Ratface, the former seated beside him and the latter in the back. And in all this time, not one policeman had looked their way. Attention was on the building; and, of course, there were plenty of other cars in the parking lot.

He did not speak now. He nosed the car forward and eased it toward the gate; one hand on the steering wheel, the other holding the gun. Ratface spoke.

"We can't—we can't—"

"Shut yer fucking mouth," Charles snarled. He drove on.

A slow approach was undoubtedly the best bet. The rifle-armed policeman was on the far side of the blocking car, speaking with the one who had just moved it. The man who watched them come, a constable from one of the squad cars, clearly thought it was a party of visitors, or doctors or something, on the move and unaware of drama going on around. Unarmed, he signaled quite casually, and Charles slowed almost to a stop before stepping suddenly on the pedal, to shoot up gravel from the back wheels. You can still see the ruts he dug.

And now Plonker and Ratface had their little moment. It was all too much for them, they had decided what Arnold decided long ago: better the mercy of the court on a relatively minor charge than wind up party to the shooting of a copper, or something. It had all gone wrong, the mad bastards' plan; and the Old Bill knew they had guns, or they couldn't have brought their own. This could mean life.

Quite independently, they acted in unison. Couldn't have done it had Charles been sitting in the back, covering them both; but Charles was in the driving seat. As he accelerated, Plonker went for the gun exactly as Ratface lunged from the back and smashed the Londoner's face forward into the steering wheel.

Poor Plonker. He grabbed the gun by the muzzle, and it blasted the two middle fingers clean off his left hand. When he plays piano now in prison concerts, critics comment upon a certain lack of thickness in his bass chording. The bullet went on to shatter Charles's kneecap as his nose smashed on the steering wheel. The car zigzagged wildly and buckled itself and the minivan, just outside the gate. Nobody sustained further injury, thank God. It was not traveling very fast.

16

That the police should believe the whole affair revolved around some kind of hot-car caper is not so surprising as it may seem. For one thing, nothing in it jogged them to connection with the bypass robbery; accepted from the start as one that went wrong, the jeweler having confirmed that his stock was all there. As he had to, and swallow the loss. He died not long after, incidentally, babbling about a fortune stolen from him, he believed by the police. Nobody took any notice, he'd been a bit funny of late. His manager is working now in Southgate. Same line of business.

Consider also the car Vennor had been driving. And Hagger's, left in the hospital car park. And the one Georgie left in the town square. All stolen.

Then again: the protagonists were not talking. Only Ratface could, in the immediate aftermath, with any degree of coherence. Later, under interrogation, they obeyed the good pro's cardinal rule: give the bastards nothing. As nobody mentioned the bypass job they kept shtum. Trouble enough they had without inviting charges of implication in a previous armed attack. The pigs insisted it was a car racket—fair enough.

Even when the Londoners were identified as very big boys indeed, nobody wondered seriously why they would concern themselves in a small-town car caper.

Hagger was in every kind of lurk; and the car caper is very, very lucrative, networked all over the country. Millions of pounds' worth of trucks and high-quality cars find their way to the Continent every year.

As for the two tearaways: no hint to be gained from them. So far as they were concerned, the car job was done, paid for, and completely forgotten, they having other matters to think about. Billy never even heard about the hospital fracas; and Mike, hearing that Vennor was involved, decided as the others had: keep shtum. Nobody has ever questioned him about it, so shtum he is to this day. He couldn't tell much, anyway, never having made mental connection between that jalopy and the raid that killed Vennor. Never did know what the cargo was.

An oddity to the case: the Hagger and Vennor lads never suspected that while they awaited trial the two tearaways hard-sought all that time were also awaiting trial, for killing a black boy. And neither tearaway suspected that the men who did for Vennor were, some of them, with him at the barn that night. Probably neither side ever will know. They are now in different prisons, they've never even met.

All the conjecture, the interrogation, the probing, the trials were in the future, of course, when Detective Inspector Cruse (he was the man in the suit who walked into the hospital beside a uniformed man with a rifle) went to see Detective Inspector Rosher, at the latter's request. As soon as he finished taking statements and seeing the mess cleared up, he went straight in.

They'd tucked Rosher back in his old bed, with new bandages on his head. And he was quite happy to be there, rather than on a marble slab right next to Jack Hagger. Actually, his injuries were not serious—the bullet that carved a hole in his hat removed a length of skin along with the hair, and he gave his potted leg a nasty twist—but in view of his previous head injury they popped him back in bed and waited to see if he'd go gaga.

Cruse said, putting on his good smile, "You look comfortable. They tell me you want to see me." And Rosher advanced his belief that the whole thing was tied to a stolen-car racket. Cruse heard him, and remarked, "Bit extreme, isn't it? I mean—armed shoot-outs and all."

"Suggest you put a trace on the car Vennor was driving," Rosher said. "Vauxhall, I believe. Out of character. And Arnold Gutte's involved. Friend of Cauliflower Davis. And Cauliflower was in here. Looking for Vennor. Said he owed him on a car deal."

"Cauliflower's dead. Got himself drowned."

"Uh-huh. Back of Vennor's garage. Soil marks to say he'd been in there. And Vennor's manager, man called Ackers. Take a look at him, he's bent."

"Have you seen him, then?" Crafty old sod—have you been nosing around?

"Just called in. Passing the time."

So there you are: once again, it was Rosher who helped to point the course of the inquiry. Because if none of his colleagues ever sent him valentines, when he advanced a tip they followed it up. It would be solid.

Young Alec Cruse, his legman often in days gone by, had good reason to respect his professional ability. Wherefore, from one of the patrol cars at the hospital gate (the minibus was hors de combat) he radioed for a check on Vennor's car and learned that it was now at that man's garage. Mrs. Vennor had instructed that it be towed there, and left.

Right, he thought: there's your reason for calling. Let's go and have a look around. Strike while the flak's flying. He coined the odd air force cliché. His hobby was stick-it-yourself plastic aircraft kits.

He rode in the back of one of the squad cars to Vennor's place, and the manager took on a greenish glisten when he saw a muscular man and two big policemen, all advancing on his office. He said, "Ah. Ahah. Good afternoon—er—gentlemen."

"Good afternoon, sir," said Young Alec, thinking: The old sod's right. Bent, and scared with it. "Detective Inspector Cruse. I believe you have a car here. A Vauxhall, belonging to Mr. Vennor.

"Mr. Vennor's in the hospital—"

"Mr. Vennor is dead, sir. We'll see the car, if you please."

It was one of the uniformed men who recognized Collie's car, standing on the concrete close by the smashed Vauxhall. Collie lived on his cruising patch, and a policeman by routine familiarizes himself with the transport attached to his own personal villains. Cruse asked the manager, "How does this car come to be here, sir?"

"We're awaiting instructions," Mr. Ackers said; and out on the oily scrapyard the boy Albert attached his magnets to the newly stripped carcass of that jalopy. Syd collected it before lunch, whipped out the engine and everything of value, and returned it scagged and bent a little for disguise's sake. Not that he'd needed to bother, the boy Albert and the man Sam were, as Mr. Ackers had believed, both too dumb to recognize it. "The owner—"

"The owner is also dead, sir. A Mr. Davis, drowned behind your yard."

"Ah," said Mr. Ackers. "Ah. Well, in that case—"

There was a plain girl working there. She made the tea, put things into files, stuck on stamps, even answered the phone, when pressed. She came out now and spoke. " 'Scuse me, Mr. Ackers. Is this gentleman Detective Cruse?" Her eyes were fixed upon Cruse in awed wonder. She'd never seen a detective before. Not in the flesh. He was even better looking than Starsky. *And* Hutch.

"I'm Cruse," said Cruse.

"Oo. There's a phone call for you."

"Thank you."

Oo, she could fancy that. What were they doing here? Oo—look at the other two. She could fancy them, too, but of course they weren't detectives. Ooo...

Cruse had told the station where he would be. Finding the patrol-car radio unmanned, they'd rung through. Swansea said that the license number on the Vauxhall belonged by right to a Commer van, property of Cyril Henry Taylor, 15 St. Alban's Court, Bradford, West Yorkshire.

False plates. So: very fishy car. Very fishy driver. Mr. Ackers had entered the office. So had the uniformed boys. The plain girl hovered, where she could lust unseen. Cruse addressed Mr. Ackers.

"It seems your boss's car was stolen, sir. The Vauxhall he was driving. May I ask what you know about that?"

Shock added to the green glisten. It had been puzzling Mr. Ackers, that car. Why was Vennor driving a Vauxhall? Where was the Rolls? And now: what was the bastard doing in a hot car? Events were knocking the wind out of him. He'd been worrying about that Renault engine, and all his other bits and pieces of private enterprise.

Cruse was watching his face. Attack now. This was the time. "I think, sir," he said, "that we should have a little talk. Don't you? Perhaps, if you have somebody to take over here, you will accompany me to the station."

Oo, said the plain girl. Oo ooooo...

So, you see, even Mr. Ackers confirmed in the police mind the belief that their inquiries should center on Vennor's involvement in a car caper. Because:

Car salesmen may lack all sorts of moral qualities, but they do possess agile wits. Cruse escorted Mr. Ackers from the premises just as Old Bob with the wobbly eye removed the jalopy from his crusher squashed into a neat pack like an oversize bouillon cube, jewels and all. By the time he reached the station, the manager had prayed, and received guidance.

Vennor was dead. He couldn't argue. Vennor was driving a hot car. So: all the funny little things that must come to light now that the police really were sniffing, he had done at Vennor's instigation.

Within an hour, he was cooperating; but saying nothing about the jalopy with the Renault engine, because that came up after Vennor was hospitalized. He talked of cars rigged, clocks turned back, duplicate books. Of the system that filled his tanks with two-star petrol and sold it out as four-star. Oh, many things. Enough to stamp Vennor well and truly bent.

But he knew nothing, he swore, about a bigger car racket. He believed Vennor might well have been involved in one, he was capable, all right—had to say that; the blacker he painted Vennor, the better—but if he was he operated it from elsewhere. He, Mr. Ackers, knew nothing about that. And he kept quiet about Syd. Syd would help him to get set up again, when he came out. Vennor handled everything through his own contacts, he said. Very close man.

Well—it worked, from his point of view. Largely as the result of his ready—nay, enthusiastic—cooperation with the police, he only drew six months. He is back in the business now, and being very careful. You may buy from him with confidence.

TAILPIECE

On the following evening, Detective Inspector Rosher lay in his bed well content. He was in no particular pain, and gratified to find himself once more a bit of a hero. The television news people had been in, and the press; and the chief constable. Who issued mild reproof against his having discharged himself from here last time around. Mild, because what can you say to a man who captures and beats into harmlessness an armed criminal, working in his own time from crutches with his leg in plaster and a crease in the top of his head? And then points to an obvious car racket. This chief always had favored Rosher, anyway. It made Percy Fillimore spit.

But Rosher, lying comfortably back against the pillows which Nurse Holness had just repositioned for him, was not thinking of Percy Fillimore. He was thinking of life in general, and of how pleasant it had become. He was thinking of her.

She had been televised, too. She was in all the papers, because the arrest of two youths for the murder of her brother was already news. She had submitted quietly to the pestering, the insolent patronizing, the positioning alongside Rosher so that they could appear together while a perfumed pouf from the BBC asked banal questions. She had worked all day, very quietly, withdrawn from her natural West Indian ebullience. She had been very attentive to Rosher. She was here now, his pillows freshly resettled, doing things to his bedside cupboard that didn't need doing.

She must like me, he thought. And I'm not that old. There've been people older than me settled down with people younger than her. And nurses are not flibber-tigibbets, they don't giggle all the time. Sod it—she must like me, or she wouldn't be in here. He asked, "How long am I going to be stuck here?"

"Until we let you out, this time." She smiled. Sod it—she *must* like him, or she wouldn't smile.

"Well—when I'm out I'll—take you to dinner. Somewhere nice."

"Thank you," she said.

"You earned it. Saved my life, didn't you?"

"Killed a man, really, didn't I?"

"Man with a gun, he was using it."

"Still a man. Still killed him."

"Wouldn't upset yourself about that. They'll probably give you a medal for it." They very well might. A nurse, and a colored one, saving a white policeman— and her brother just murdered. Oh yes—they most likely would give her a medal.

"Big deal." She moved to the door; and beyond his natural male appreciation of buttock and breast and cleanly feminine rustling something deeper was singing in him—the something that mixes tenderness and sex to a solution far more dangerous to a man than uncomplicated lust. He watched her go, thinking: Of course, it will lead to problems. But sod it—I retire next year. They've been sniggering about me for years. Let the bastards snigger.

And then he saw something quite unexpected.

As she turned left out the door, enter right a black man, handsome, tall, and young. Perhaps he was standing there already, waiting to spring his ambush, because his hands went out to touch her shoulders. She turned; and sod it—she was in his arms, head gone back to accept his kiss, eagerly. His hand, the one nearest to Rosher, moved to cup and press her breast. Her soft, desirable breast.

She came from the kiss; her eyes found Rosher, watching. She broke the hand away, hurriedly; stepped back; spoke softly. The man looked at the inspector, grinned widely, and winked. She said something more. He answered, grinning, and vanished. Reappeared. Called to the inspector with a bigger, whiter grin, "Get well soon, man." Winked again, and was gone.

Nurse Holness came back in. Some of her sparkle was on her. She said, laughing, "You weren't supposed to see that, got carried away." Women do, in times of severe strain. It moves them sexually. "I've told him time and again not to come for me at work, Sister'd have a fit if she'd seen that, kissing and all. But he got tired of waiting downstairs, I'm a quarter hour overtime, Lynn hasn't turned up yet. Five-thirty, I should have finished."

"Who is he?" Rosher asked. She'd said she was busy this evening. He had not really been noticing, at the time.

"Hector? My fiancé."

"I didn't know you were engaged."

"Not were, *am*. You didn't ask."

"Hrrm," said Rosher. "Grrrrmph." He reached to his locker for the enormous off-white handkerchief. Experienced by now, she left the room quietly, closing the door to keep the trump of mad elephants in. When he had mopped up, the inspector spent the rest of the evening glowering at the ceiling.

Oh yes—and a few days later, all those neat metal packages were collected by truck from Vennor's garage, in the way of legitimate trade, and transported to the foundry in the big city, where—it is the glorious resurrection for all old cars; may it come likewise to us—they are melted down and re-formed into sheet metal, for a fresh lease of life as spanking new vehicles fit again to be worshiped and wax-polished, world without end, amen.

Perhaps you have never seen a foundry. The working principle is simple. The molten metal flows away, all the impurities in the raw material being left in the form of slurry; which flows by its own channel into tanks, or trucks, for dumping. Nobody inspects the slurry, to see if there are tiny little lumps in it. Who cares, with slurry?